The Red Lion

The Red Lion

by NEIL STEWART

Illustrated by
JOSEPH CELLINI

G. P. PUTNAM'S SONS
NEW YORK

Published simultaneously in the Dominion of Canada
by Longmans, Green and Company, Toronto

Library of Congress
Catalogue Card Number: 60-12538

Manufactured in the United States of America
Van Rees Press • New York

CONTENTS

*To Don McGiffin, whose ancestors followed
the banner of the Bruce.*

The Man with Yellow Hair

Hugh Gordon of Glenbirnie wiggled his tired feet in their soft deerskin brogues as he sat beside the high road leading to Ayr in Galloway. Absently he scratched the black ears of a small Border sheep dog sprawled across his knee-length green tunic.

"Maybe we've walked too far, Jamie. Three miles we've tramped from the hall at Glenbirnie. We'd best turn back before we meet the English!"

The small black and white dog licked the boy's face with lavish affection, but Hugh Gordon did not laugh as usual or throw a stick to be fetched. He knew he should not have ventured so far from home, for this year of 1307 was a troubled time for Scotland and Robert Bruce, the Scottish king who had become a hunted outlaw.

English men-at-arms swaggered up and down the countryside, punishing without mercy any Scot who dared oppose them. Only those of high birth who betrayed their country to the enemy were safe from English wrath.

This Hugh knew to be true, for his father had talked to him as if he were old enough to bear arms, although he was only thirteen. The boy had not forgotten Gavin Gordon's counsel as they sat by the fire in the great hall at Glenbirnie. "There's nothing a lad like you can do to help Robert Bruce, who is Galloway-bred like yourself. Every castle in Scotland is held by the English or by Scots turncoats, men who have sold out their country."

"But why have our nobles betrayed Robert Bruce, Father?" Hugh had asked.

"Because they're selfish, lad, the kind who love gold more than honor. They have manors and estates on the English side of the Border." Gavin Gordon had held his lame leg to the warmth of the fire, shaking his head. "In every country and in every generation, there have been men like that, who care only for themselves. They turn with the tide. Be not like them, son. Remember you are a Gordon of Glenbirnie."

Now, as he sat by the side of the highway to Ayr, with the spring sun warming his face and glinting on Jamie's white ruff, it was hard to believe that the troubles his father had talked about so gravely were real or near.

Ever since his father had been lamed by a fall from his horse, Hugh had stayed close to Glenbirnie, missing sorely the deep woods of Glen Trool, where small brooks or burns ran swiftly down to meet the cold and crystal-clear loch which the English called a lake.

"Let's go through the forest, Jamie," he suggested. But Jamie did not dash off, bounding in circles as usual. Hugh saw the thick shoulders of the small collie stiffen as he caught the sound of hoofbeats far down the highway.

He scrambled to his feet and caught Jamie by the ruff as a dozen riders rounded the bend and galloped toward him. Hugh knew they were English on their way to Ayr, for no true Scot dared to show himself openly as long as Robert Bruce's small army was hiding in the Glen Trool region, heavily outnumbered by the enemy.

Hugh gripped his staff firmly and stood his ground as the party halted. The leader, a heavily built man in a mail shirt, pulled in his horse sharply and ignored Jamie's threatening growl.

"Who are you, boy?"

"My name is Hugh Gordon, sir." The good manners taught him at St. Cuthbert's priory where he went to school were evident.

"You talk like a monk," the Englishman sneered. He inspected Hugh closely, noting the black hair, the Norman nose and blue eyes above the sensitive mouth. "How old are you?"

"Thirteen, sir."

"And a loyal Scot, I doubt not."

"And a loyal Scot," Hugh replied stoutly.

"Then I suppose you could tell where Robert Bruce hides. The outlaw you call king!"

"Sir, everyone knows King Robert is here in Galloway where he was born. Even the English know that."

The Englishman's eyes turned frosty in his ruddy face. "You're but a lad. Guard your tongue as you grow older, lest you dance a jig on the scaffold. King Robert! Bah!"

He sank spurs in his black charger and the troop galloped away. A man-at-arms in the last file bent down as he rode past and thrust his spear at Jamie, narrowly missing the dog's body.

Hugh grabbed the little collie in his arms and hugged him to his chest as raucous laughter echoed down the

dusty highway. Only when the English riders had disappeared did the boy feel some of the tautness go out of
him. The deep-pitted growls of the dog ceased. Hugh put
Jamie down and walked slowly into the forest of Glen
Trool, where tall oaks and birches interlaced their branches
over his head like a window to the sky.

Here the grass was green and wild flowers swept a lane
of color down the glade. Above, a golden eagle circled,
floating lazily against the white clouds. Even at that distance, Hugh could make out the markings clearly, for he
had gifted eyes.

It was a never-ending wonder to his father and to the
people in the little village close to Glenbirnie that he could
see twice as far as a grown man. The monks at St. Cuthbert
always said that God had given him a great talent. Of that
Hugh was proud and often offered his thanks in the chapel
of the priory.

As he strode swiftly along the path, he thought of that
one gift he had. He thought also of the troubled land of
Scotland, of the loyalty the Gordons bore King Robert,
of the anger and pain on the face of his father whose lame
leg kept him from joining the hidden army.

Until today it had been only talk he had heard among
his elders. Now it was real. He had seen the enemy. Surely
there was something he could do for Scotland. Perhaps
the Bruce had need for a lad with eyes like his own.

Hugh called Jamie sharply to heel. He was no longer a
boy in the woods with his dog, looking for a boy's adventure, with a sharp knife tucked into his brown leather belt.
The pretending was over. Somewhere in the forest was
Robert Bruce and his small army. He knew now he meant
to find the outlawed king.

The woods were silent, except for the chattering of small
birds and the sound of the burn brawling its way over

sandstone to the River Ayr. The forest was peaceful as the nave of a great cathedral.

Hugh glanced up at the sun, still high in the sky. There was still time to search for King Robert. He hesitated a moment while Jamie sat down on his haunches and looked up inquiringly.

My father will use a birch rod on me when he finds out where I've been. I'll have to eat oat bread and water for a week. I won't get to ride my horse. Swiftly Hugh weighed the consequences of what he was doing. No, he told himself. It will be worth it if I find King Robert.

On he went, his deerskin shoes a faint whisper on the green forest path. He had met no one since he left the road. There would be no English on these faint trails, for they knew enough to stay on the main road and to travel heavily armed. Otherwise, they would end up dead. To the loyal Scots, all followers of the English king, Edward II, were rogues and murderers.

Hugh had no idea where to look for an outlaw king, but he was certain he would find Robert Bruce deeper in the forest. And he would know him if he saw him, for Hugh had seen him crowned at Scone.

As Jamie trotted patiently at his heels through the forest of Glen Trool, Hugh remembered all the glory and splendor of that day at Scone. Isabella MacDuff, Countess of Buchan, had placed the gold crown on the king's head. Robert Wishart, bishop of Glasgow, had blessed the Bruce. Knights in glittering armor and beautiful ladies of the court had watched.

But, most of all, Hugh Gordon remembered the face of the king. Many times he had described it to his father whose eyes could not span the distance across the great crowd at Scone. Robert Bruce was a tall and broad-shouldered man with yellow hair and sparkling blue eyes. His smile had been tinged with sadness, not for himself but for war-ravaged Scotland. Hugh had never forgotten.

Now the king was in Galloway, hidden somewhere on the rocky slopes which led down to Glen Trool, perhaps underground in some quiet cave. Hugh hastened his steps as the sun edged toward the west.

As he half ran, half walked down the narrow trail he came to a glen through which a small burn trickled lazily. Great oak trees surrounded the green meadow beside the brook, a meadow which had been close cropped by sheep. A vast stillness filled the place. Hugh stopped short, his eyes carefully searching the broad expanse of green. He sensed the presence of a stranger.

Finally Hugh's keen eyes located the intruder. In a clump of hazel on a hillside above the glen stood a knight wearing a coat of mail. He was without a helmet, leaning on his tall shield which bore a white cross on a blue field.

Hugh was puzzled. Ordinarily a knight carried his family coat of arms on his shield. But this stranger did not want to identify himself, for his shield bore only the cross of St. Andrew, Scotland's patron saint.

Whistling softly to Jamie, Hugh stepped boldly down the path below the hillside, his heart beating faster. As he walked toward the strange knight, the man with the St. Andrew's cross on his shield turned and looked in Hugh's direction. Now he could see the stranger clearly. A tall man of powerful figure, with long yellow hair and deep blue eyes!

The boy's heart tightened. He could not be mistaken. This was King Robert! Normally he would be wearing on his shield the Red Lion of Scotland on a golden field. But a king surrounded by dangerous enemies could not afford to display the scarlet mark of his rank, his own coat of arms.

Hugh was not surprised that the Bruce carried a bow in his right hand, for unlike the English nobles, he was a famous archer. No doubt the king was looking for game, even though no hunting dogs accompanied him. The baying of hounds chasing a stag might well bring English men-at-arms hot on his trail.

Hugh's excitement rose as he broke into a trot toward the king, with Jamie close behind. He saw Robert Bruce watching him with lowered bow. I am just a lad, Hugh thought, with only a knife at my belt. Of course he is not afraid of me.

As he neared King Robert, he slowed his pace. Then, a few feet away from the royal presence, he fell on one knee, as he had seen knights at Scone do. Even Jamie stilled his wagging tail and was silent.

King Robert's watchful face changed. "Who are you, lad?"

"Hugh Gordon of Glenbirnie, sire, and a loyal Scot."

The king's face softened. "Rise, Hugh Gordon. I am glad to meet a loyal Scot. There are too few of us."

Hugh stood, his blue eyes alight. This was his king. Here was his chance to serve. He spoke with eager respect. "Your Majesty's pardon, but I have information. English men-at-arms are close to Glen Trool. A dozen galloped by me two short hours ago, riding toward Ayr."

The king's face was stern. "Yes, I am surrounded by the English—and by disloyal Scots. But they keep their distance. They fear the lion's claws." King Robert smiled again. "But how did you know me, lad? Have you ever seen me before?"

"Yes, sire, at Scone. I was twelve, and my father took me to see Your Highness crowned."

"You are of gentlefolk, lad. What is your father's name?"

"Gavin Gordon of Glenbirnie, sire. A Galloway manor."

"Oh, yes, I remember now. I am a Galloway man, too. I have not seen Gordon of Glenbirnie for many years. It was told me that he was sorely ill."

"He is lame, sire. A fall from his charger four years ago. Otherwise, he would be here, sword in hand, fighting for his rightful king."

The king's eyes flashed. "Would that all Scots were like the Gordons of Glenbirnie! Tell your father that I asked about him, that he has my love and affection."

"Thank you, sire." Hugh looked up at the tall king and hesitated. "Your Majesty," he said slowly, "I would serve with thee. As a page, belike, since I am of gentle blood."

King Robert eyed Hugh's compact, sturdy figure under the green tunic. "How old are you, Hugh?"

"I'll be fourteen, come Christmas."

The king was tactful. "I am sure you could be of great service to me, lad. But your father, what of him? He is lame, as you say. Should you not stay at Glenbirnie and keep him company?"

"Maybe I should," Hugh said slowly. "He has only old Thomas Dickson and his wife there. Except when my cousin, Alan Gordon, visits us." Hugh scowled. "He is my kinsman, but him I do not like."

"Why not, lad?"

Hugh hesitated. "He is—what you, sire, would call disloyal. One of the Scots who is leagued with the English against you. He is the only Gordon like that, Your Majesty. Take me, sire. I would serve you well."

King Robert seated himself on a granite boulder beside the trail. "Get thee down at my feet, lad, and we will talk. Things are beginning to come back to me. Your mother was a Ferguson."

"Why, yes, sire." Hugh's amazement showed in his eyes.

King Robert smiled. "We are distant kinsmen, then.

Both of us descended from Fergus, last of the Celtic princes of Galloway. You speak Gaelic?"

"A little, sire. My nurse taught me. I speak French also. The brothers at St. Cuthbert's pounded it into my head."

"Good, good, lad. What else is there to recommend you to me?"

Hugh thought for a few seconds. "Why, sire, I can see great distances. Perhaps you could use someone like me?"

The king was thoughtful. "Lad, this war will be a long one, and you are young. I intend to fight here and to die— if need be." The king's eyes flashed in anger. "Do you know what this war is about, Hugh Gordon? A war to prevent big and greedy England from swallowing up little Scotland. A small nation has the right to exist side by side with a powerful neighbor. We are fighting for that right.

"I have been hunted from Scotland to Ireland and back again. My queen is a prisoner of the English. So is my daughter, the Princess Marjory. Three of my four brothers have been sent to the headsman's ax. But I shall fight on, and some day I will conquer, even as David conquered Goliath. And, when I do, I hope to have Hugh Gordon at my side."

"I am ready, sire, now." Hugh had leaped to his feet, ready to fight on the instant.

"Go back to Glenbirnie, Hugh." The king's voice was soft. "Honor God and serve thy father. Practice in the tilt-yard. Learn how to use sword and lance, to bend the bow. Fit thyself for the hard struggle ahead. Come to me a year, two years hence. I shall make you my page—even my squire—if you desire it."

"I do, sire, I do."

Hugh knelt on one knee and kissed the king's hand. "I shall go now, sire. God guard thee." He looked down the

glen where Jamie was chasing squirrels. Far in the distance, he could see three men walking toward the king,
their pace deliberate. Hugh could sense evil in his bones.
These men coming toward King Robert were like hunters
who had already flushed their quarry.

"Your Highness," Hugh said, "three approach from the
west. The man in the middle is one-eyed, and he bears
a bow. Another has a sword, another an ax. They look
like ruffians, sire."

King Robert turned quickly and looked toward the
newcomers. He shook his head. "I can barely see them.
Truly, you have wondrous eyes. Give me my bow, lad."

Hugh placed the big bow carefully in the king's hand
and put the royal shield down on the boulder. Slowly
the strangers walked forward, until their voices could be
heard. "Hola! Sir Knight! We mean thee no harm. We
be poor peasants hunting hares."

"Does one hunt hares with a sword?" King Robert
muttered. "Boy, you have rare eyes. Tell me what you
see."

"The one-eyed man, a huge rascal, is drawing an arrow
from his quiver. He will make a long shot."

"My thanks, Hugh Gordon. Take the dog and run home.
Fast." The king's voice was so stern Hugh turned on his
heel and dashed back on the trail toward the high road.

Some fifteen yards away, he turned and looked back.
King Robert stood quietly, arrow on string. He had not
yet bent the bow.

Farther away, Hugh could see the three men advancing
on their prey. The one-eyed peasant in the middle called
out loudly, "I know thee, sire. I am a true Scot. Who
should be nearer thy person than I?"

As he spoke, he drew the bowstring back with practiced
hand. But the king was quicker. The arrow left Bruce's

bended bow on lightning flight. The one-eyed man fell forward into the long grass.

King Robert picked up his shield and, sword in hand, rushed forward to meet the other two. Hugh saw the peasant with the ax swing and miss. The king cut him down, then turned to meet the lone survivor.

The fight was brief. King Robert caught the peasant's sword on his shield, deflecting the blade. Then Bruce made one short, deadly thrust, and the man dropped to the ground.

Hugh watched the king standing motionless, leaning on his blue and silver shield. Then he turned and lifted his gauntleted hand in salute. While Jamie ran ahead of him, Hugh raised his own hand like a knight in full armor and raced toward Glenbirnie as though his brown brogues wore wings.

For a boy who had aided his king, he knew full well there would be no birch rod that night, and no oat bread and water.

Glenbirnie Castle

arkness had fallen long before Hugh reached the rise of ground near the little lake everyone in Galloway called Loch Urr. As he saw the beams of light coming from the slitted windows high up in the walls of the castle's keep, the boy suddenly realized that his feet were weary and the day had been long.

He looked at Jamie who was too tired to chase imaginary rabbits. "It's hungry I am clear to my ankles and thirsty to my thumbs!" He tightened his belt and hurried on until he could make out the dim outlines of the castle with its surrounding wall sitting majestically on a small peninsula jutting into the lake.

Filled with a longing for a beef joint and almost bursting with his own importance at meeting the king, Hugh trotted over the drawbridge, left Jamie in the empty courtyard, and bounded up the worn stone steps.

As he threw open the heavy oaken doors of the great hall, he welcomed the familiar warmth of the long, wide room, dimly lighted by candles set in wall brackets. The fire in the circular fireplace in the middle of the hall threw its flickering light on the rush-strewn floor.

His father's voice from the big oak chair was stern. "Where have you been, young rascal? It's long past the supper hour."

Hugh moved quickly to his father's side, looking down at the white hair with a lump in his throat. His father had been a strong man a few years ago. Now he seemed old and broken.

Because of the sorrow, Hugh spoke gently. "Something wonderful happened to me today, Father. I was walking through the forest of Glen Trool and I met King Robert. I even talked to him, sir!"

Swiftly Gavin Gordon raised a warning finger to his lips.

From the hallway came a familiar voice. "Say you so, young cousin. I had not realized that Bruce was so close by. Nor that Hugh Gordon was his friend."

Alan Gordon sauntered into the room. He was bald, thin and angular, his face pinched, his mouth sharp. He eyed the boy with hawklike interest. "Tell me more, cousin. Was your king well fed and happy when last you saw him? Maybe you could tell where he bides."

The contempt in Alan Gordon's voice convinced Hugh his kinsman had no right to be treated with the courtesy of a guest.

"I will tell you nothing," he said shortly.

Alan Gordon ignored the rebuff. "Perhaps I should report this happening to the commander of the English garrison at Dumfries."

Gavin Gordon's eyes smoldered, his fingers closing tightly around his thick cane. "Have done, Alan. The boy knows naught of Robert Bruce. He is telling a tale."

"Not so, Cousin Gavin. No Gordon is a liar. Young cousin, you have been keeping company with an outlaw, if you met Robert Bruce."

"I tell you the boy is mistaken," Gavin Gordon protested, fear crowding his eyes.

Hugh understood now. His father was desperately trying to shield him. One word from Alan about his adventure and the English would question him closely. He might even be thrown into the dungeon at Dumfries.

Casually Alan picked up his sword leaning against a wall and belted it on. "I must take my leave now, cousin. Perhaps the lad was mistaken. Of a certainty you can depend on me not to betray him. I did but jest about telling the English."

Gavin Gordon lifted his hand in farewell to his unwelcome guest. "I give you good even. Lad, light Cousin Alan to his horse."

"Yes, Father." Hugh walked ahead of his cousin, pausing to take a candle from its sconce on the wall. He opened the great door and stepped out into the night with Alan Gordon, who shouted loudly until his sleepy groom led two horses from the stable below.

Hugh held the candle high while Alan Gordon mounted and looked down with a smooth smile and unreadable eyes. "Thou art a lad of spirit, Hugh. But do not roam so far away from Glenbirnie. It might be dangerous."

The boy listened to the hoofbeats die away beyond the drawbridge. He knew he had not heard the last of Cousin Alan. The man now held a whip hand and kinship meant nothing. If only he had looked around before he blurted out his great adventure to his father.

A voice came from the stable door. "Is it thou, lad?"

"Aye, Thomas." He went to meet the tall, straight man with the white hair who long ago had taught him to fish and swim and ride. He knew Thomas Dickson in his younger days had been a stout man-at-arms, expert with shield and sword as well as the bow.

"So they've gone at last," the old man observed. "And a good riddance. That groom is as insolent as an Englishman."

"And so is his master, albeit he is my own kin. I think I have today brought trouble on the keep, Thomas." Briefly he told the old man what had happened in the great hall. "I am young, as the king said, but you must teach me all you know of tilting and drawing the longbow. In a year I must be ready to join the Bruce."

"I will teach you well, lad," Thomas promised as Hugh gave him a hand in lowering the portcullis. When the heavy iron-barred gate swung down into place before the metal-faced oaken gates, the old man looked grave. "May God protect us. You are young and the master and I are old."

Hugh bade him good night and made his way soberly to the great hall. His father still sat by the fireplace waiting. "Has he gone, lad?"

"Aye, Father. I have been helping Thomas lower the portcullis."

"And now," Gavin Gordon said, "he will go to one of the two watchtowers above the castle and keep a sharp watch as he has for forty years past. Glenbirnie has fallen on evil times. Yet Thomas remains loyal. There are only two of us left now."

Hugh knew what his father meant. Hugh's older brother had been killed at Falkirk. Hugh's mother had died soon after. Truly his father was right. Only two Gordons remained. Two Gordons and old Thomas to guard Glenbirnie.

Gavin Gordon shifted in his chair. "Did Alan say naught to you as he left?"

"Yes sir. He told me not to roam too far afield lest I encounter danger."

"That is true, but there is a greater danger closer to Glenbirnie and to you. I do not trust Alan Gordon even though our grandfathers were brothers. He would sell out his kinfolk for English gold. He could do you mortal harm, lad."

"It is my fault, Father. I should not have spoken of the king. I did not know Cousin Alan was here. But truly I did meet the Bruce. He asked about you and sent you his love and affection. Those were his very words."

Gavin Gordon looked pleased. "That was kind of the Bruce. I knew him well in my younger days, but in recent years our paths have not crossed. This leg forbids me to do battle as I would wish."

"That is not all, Father. I did the king a service with my eyes." Hugh told his story well, leaving out no detail, watching his father's face anxiously when he asked permission to serve his king in a year.

Gavin Gordon stared long into the dying fire, then put his hand on the boy's head. "I cannot go myself, but you seek the Bruce, lad, if you wish. You are young, but your gifted eyes will serve him well. Now, help me to bed, son. The day has been long. Your supper is by the kitchen hearth. You have about you a hungry look!"

The cool, clear air of an April morning came in through the open window of Hugh's sleeping room with the first rays of the sun. He threw off the wool blanket and put his feet down hard on the bare stone floor.

Hurriedly he dressed, first the undershirt of wool, next a clean tunic, finally the long brown hose. Slipping his feet into the brogues, he hastened to the oak chest that held a basin and a pitcher of water. The water was cold to his face, and he caught up a rough towel, rubbing his cheeks vigorously. Suddenly he realized he was hungry and hurried down to the great hall, reaching it just as his father limped out of his bedroom.

Hugh greeted the elder Gordon and sat beside him at the table which stood on a platform nine inches above the floor of the hall. Meg Dickson put a mound of steaming oatcakes before them and reached into the oaken cupboard for pewter cups and plates.

When she came back with eggs and fried trout on another platter, Hugh ate as only a growing boy can, drinking wine diluted with water from his cup.

Finally his father pushed back the plate. "What do you plan today, lad? Not another visit to the forest of Glen Trool, I hope."

"No, indeed, sir. This morning I will practice swordplay, if Thomas is of a mind to teach me."

"He will. Old Thomas is a famous sworder." Gavin Gordon glanced at the wall before him, where a blade hung in its scabbard. "Take that sword, son. It is lighter than most, fit for the hand of a boy who is not quite a man."

"Thank you, Father." Hugh reached for the scabbard and pulled out the sword, marveling at its light weight, symmetry and beauty. It was almost three inches shorter than the average Scottish blade, which was wide at the hilt, tapering slightly to the point. This blade was much narrower, with a keen cutting edge.

In high excitement, Hugh rushed into the courtyard to

find Thomas Dickson. At last he was to practice with a real sword!

"Thomas," he called. "My father has given me a sword, and time wastes!"

The old man smiled at Hugh's impatience. "Aye. I'll teach you to use it well. Come and get Rufus. He's fair champing at the bit."

Inside the stables Hugh's big red horse gave him a boisterous welcome. Thomas Dickson placed the high-horned leather saddle on his back and slipped the bridle into the stallion's mouth. Hugh led him out of the stall. Rufus was sixteen hands high, too tall for a boy, but Hugh prided himself on riding a horse stout enough to carry a knight with the heaviest armor imaginable.

In the long tiltyard, he dismounted and tied the red horse to the fence. Then he looked at the oak posts six feet high, their wood bearing the scars of savage slashes. Here young squires who would be knights had practiced, wielding the sword against posts which could not strike back. But Hugh knew there were no young squires left from the generation of his grandfather, when Glenbirnie Castle had sheltered twenty men-at-arms.

Thomas did not dwell on the past. "Get busy, lad. Work up a sweat."

Hugh walked to within a few feet of the nearest oak post, drew his sword and sank the blade deep into the wood. Pulling it out, he struck again and again.

As he cut at the post, he walked around and around it, striking higher, simulating a knight who had been de-horsed and must defend himself from an enemy still on horseback. Hugh kept up his strokes doggedly for half an hour before his arms could no longer lift the sword. Sweat ran in a steady stream from his neck and bare arms.

Old Thomas watched thoughtfully. "Rest for a few minutes, lad."

Hugh threw himself on the grass, disgusted. "I guess I wouldn't last long in a battle!"

"You have sturdy enough shoulders, boy, and long arms. You will make a swordsman. Not today, but in a year if you practice faithfully."

"Think you, Thomas, that I could ever master the lance? I must do so in order to become a knight." Hugh's face was anxious.

"All in good time, lad. You must have more height. A boy your age can scarcely wield a lance."

"But I must learn quickly!"

"Why so great a hurry, young squire?"

Hugh leaned closer, his voice a whisper. "Soon, within the year, I will join King Robert. My father has said so."

"God bless the Bruce," Thomas Dickson said. "If only I were young enough to go with you! But, if you are to fight for the king, get thee into red Rufus' saddle. You must use a sword on horseback as well as on foot."

Hugh rode to the north end of the tiltyard. Setting spurs to the stallion, he dashed down the lane of oak posts. As he came to the first, he struck a blow close to the top. Rufus dashed on and Hugh, leaning down from the horse's broad back, aimed a stroke at a post on the other side. Splinters flew in all directions. He practiced his sword strokes on horseback until the sun stood high and his arm ached.

"Enough for this morning," Thomas shouted at the other end of the tiltyard. "We'll practice with the lance this afternoon."

Hugh was ravenous as Meg put the food on the table at noon. He demolished a whole grouse in short order and ate heartily of salmon and coarse wheaten bread, topped off by a venison pastry.

Gavin Gordon watched Hugh with a slight smile as the boy plied spoon and knife. "Hungry, lad? How went the swordplay?"

"I am learning, Father. This afternoon I will try the lance."

"Truly a knight's weapon, lad. Many a lance I shivered in the old days, before misfortune came to Glenbirnie."

"What misfortune, Father?"

"In your grandfather's time, the manor was five times as big as it is now. Alexander Gordon was knighted after the Battle of Largs. He was rich and powerful. But after his death, the Armstrongs influenced the king to give them part of the Glenbirnie holdings. There was naught I could do. To have resisted would have brought ruin on us all."

"I am sorry, Father." Hugh's eyes were glowing as he dropped on one knee and laid his hand on Gavin Gordon's sleeve. "Some day, sir, I will help put Robert Bruce on his throne again. When that day comes, I will gain back the land of the Gordons. I swear it."

"I believe you, lad. But do not set your heart on it. Love God, obey the king, fight to drive the invader from Scotland, and the future will take care of itself. Now get thee some rest before you use the lance. You are still a growing boy, son."

After sleeping an hour, Hugh was so sore he felt he could never get up. His arms were like lead, but he remembered he wanted to fight for King Robert and pulled himself to his feet.

He put on over his undershirt a hauberk or shirt of mail, made of leather covered with a network of chains and links, which reached to his knees. Then he took a triangular shield from the wall of his room and climbed down the ladder. In the hall below he picked up an ashwood spear ten feet long, shorter than the average lance.

Thomas Dickson was already in the tiltyard when Hugh rode Rufus into the enclosure. The old man had set up a dummy covered with coat of mail and shield on one of the oak posts.

"Ready, lad?"

"I'll try, Thomas."

Hugh set spurs to the red stallion and dashed toward the post. He tried to put the point of his light lance squarely into the iron boss of the dummy's shield, but Thomas had slanted the shield at an odd angle. The ashwood lance slipped off as Rufus galloped past.

"Try again, lad."

Once more, Hugh drove in the spurs, and Rufus leaped forward. This time Hugh struck the dummy's shield squarely, the force of his blow knocking the dummy from the post.

Hugh learned fast. Under old Thomas' expert handling, he drove himself through the misty spring and the hot summer, and well into the fall. He ate enormous meals and seemed to grow inches at a time. As he worked with sword, shield and lance, he thought often of his cousin, Alan, the false Gordon. Alan, who wanted Glenbirnie for his own, even if he had to dispossess his own blood kin.

Yes, Hugh decided, I must some day protect myself, my father, and Glenbirnie from Alan Gordon. I must learn to use every weapon well, he thought, and wondering thus about his future, he changed, almost imperceptibly, from boy to young man.

Hugh and his father celebrated Christmas together

during one of the coldest winters Galloway had ever known. Ice and sleet covered the moors and turned the hills into a new, white world.

As Hugh waited impatiently for the coming of spring, he sometimes wondered what had become of King Robert. Glenbirnie Castle was off main-traveled roads, and information was hard to come by. But he felt sure that the Bruce was still alive, even though the king and his Scots hiding in the Glen Trool region might have suffered overmuch from cold and frostbite.

When the first spring freshets began to pour down into the waters of Loch Urr, Hugh resumed his long hours of practice with sword and lance. He spent almost all of his time in the tiltyard, or at the archery butts testing his skill with the bow. He roamed the meadows and glens, looking for game. Many times he could see a hare or grouse at a great distance with his keen eyes, even though it was too far away to bring down with an arrow.

Coming back from an afternoon hunting trip early in April, he found Gavin Gordon pale with fear, his hand over his heart. Running to find Thomas, Hugh was terrified. But, when he returned to the hall, his father spoke softly. "I am all right, lad, but you are in mortal peril."

"What is wrong, Father?"

"Alan Gordon, the traitor, paid me a visit today. He has threatened to denounce you as a friend of the Bruce unless I agree to deed over to him the acres of Glenbirnie. I retain a life interest, and that is all."

"Can he do this to us, Father?"

"I am afraid he can. I am an old man, with not much life left. But you are young. As long as you are near me, Alan will watch you. He may even find a way to murder you. So get thee to the Bruce's camp. You will be safer with the king than at home. You understand that, lad?"

"Yes, Father, but I hate to leave you."

"Be not worried, lad. Thomas Dickson and his good wife Meg have been taking care of me for years. You start at dawn tomorrow, Hugh. God go with thee."

The Steps of Trool

Gavin Gordon was quiet at breakfast the next morning. Hugh ate mechanically, his mind miles away. He had what he had always wanted, permission to join the king. But now he realized how young he was, how unskilled in the grim business of war. Also he worried about his father, who had aged considerably in the past year.

Gavin Gordon broke the silence. "Lad, you should be on your way. I'll sleep easier when I know you are with King Robert."

"How will you explain my disappearance to Cousin Alan, Father?"

"He may not visit here again for six months. He has

what he wants, Glenbirnie. But if you live, lad, and if the Bruce defeats the English, you will get the manor back from Alan. Some Scots say harsh things about King Robert, but one thing no man can say, that he is disloyal to his friends."

Gavin Gordon beckoned to Meg Dickson. "Good Meg, fill a sack with food, some oatmeal, a haunch of beef, and mutton. And do not forget the skillet. Hugh is going to join his king. He will live in the open and cook for himself, like a soldier." Hugh's father sighed. "Would that I could go with thee, lad. Promise one thing, son. Be not too reckless in battle."

"I shall try to be careful, Father."

"One more thing, boy. Wear your mail shirt under your tunic. And do not carry your sword swung too openly on the saddle. You will not need a helmet, just a steel headpiece under your bonnet."

As Hugh started to protest, Gavin Gordon raised a warning hand. "I know, son, thou wouldst like to bear lance and shield and ride on a charger, like a knight in full armor. But the English would stop you on the road to Ayr if they thought your birth was gentle."

"Shall I ride Rufus, Father?"

"No, Rufus is a war horse, but much too slow if you have to run for it. Take Sheila, the little black mare. She is as surefooted as a goat."

"Aye, Father."

After breakfast Hugh climbed up to his room in the keep and he put on the coat of mail beneath his tunic. Next he took down from the wall a flat blue bonnet with a steel headpiece concealed inside. "I hope this metal saves me from a broken skull some day," he muttered. Finally he belted his sword around his waist, sighing as he did so. He did not in the least resemble a knight, rather he looked like a peasant fresh from the fields. His father was right. He would have been conspicuous wearing a visible helmet and armor.

Slowly he stepped down the ladder, glancing into the great hall where his father stood erect near the fire. He knew what it cost the elder Gordon to throw his shoulders back. Gavin Gordon was an old, bent man, honoring a son about to start on a perilous adventure.

As Hugh entered the hall, his father beckoned to him with a hand which contained a small leather pouch. "Here are twenty gold pieces, lad, which I have hoarded for years. If you are ever captured by the English, this gold may buy you your freedom."

"Thank you, Father, but I do not really need the money."

"Take it, lad," Gavin said, placing his hand on Hugh's shoulder. He touched the hilt of the blade in Hugh's scabbard. "Never draw it without cause, never sheathe it with dishonor. You understand, son?"

"Yes, Father, I do."

Gavin Gordon embraced his son. "Go now—before I weep. Thomas has Sheila in the courtyard below, with food stowed away in the saddlebags."

Hugh squeezed his father's hand and ran down to the place where Thomas Dickson stood, bareheaded, beside the little black mare. Jamie, the collie, was subdued and silent, thrusting his cold nose upward into the palm of Hugh's hand. It was hard parting from Jamie, as though he were leaving his childhood behind him.

As Hugh gathered up Sheila's reins, old Thomas solemnly shook hands. "Guard thyself in battle, young sir."

"I will do that, Thomas. Take good care of Father and Glenbirnie. Good-by, Jamie."

The little mare trotted out across the drawbridge and

into the green meadow beside the loch. Hugh turned in his saddle and looked back at Thomas Dickson and Jamie watching him. He waved and rode rapidly up the glen which led to the great Ayr highway.

He was not exactly sure where he could find King Robert and his small army. According to rumor, the Scots were hiding in the woods around Loch Doon. He decided that the best thing to do would be to cut off the Ayr highway and head west, through the forest where he had watched the king fight the three woodsmen.

Sheila reached the main road, and Hugh turned her toward Ayr. It was early morning, and few wayfarers were traveling. Now and then a shepherd with a band of sheep crossed the highway, leading his charges to greener grass on the other side. Always he was accompanied by a black and white Border collie, which made Hugh's heart ache for Jamie. C502046 CO. SCHOOLS

It wasn't long before he reached the point from which he had wandered into the forest of Glen Trool such a short year ago. He pulled over to the side of the road and munched some bread and cheese while Sheila grazed quietly.

Gathering up the reins, he looked to the north and saw a great cloud of dust moving toward him on the highway, the kind of dust usually raised by English soldiers riding recklessly and in a mortal big hurry. Hugh put the spurs to Sheila and galloped toward the crossroad a few hundred yards ahead.

The cloud of dust rolled closer, and Hugh spurred Sheila again. He had to get off that main road and into the forest before the English reached him. They were still far away, but his keen eyes caught sight of men in hauberk and helmet. He saw also, in the lead, a bulky man who looked very much like the English officer who had stopped him on that exciting day he had met King Robert! That officer, Hugh decided, might ask him questions he would be unable to answer.

Hugh looked to the side of the road as he galloped straight for the party of English soldiers. A stone fence paralleled the highway, but it was old. Some of the stones had long since crumbled, leaving openings into the meadow.

There were shouts up ahead. He saw the Englishman in the lead violently waving his arms. If they stop me, I'll be a prisoner, he thought frantically. Without slackening speed, he pulled on the bridle, and Sheila swerved sharply through a wide gap in the stone fence, almost unseating him.

Leaning over the mare's neck, he headed at top speed for the friendly shelter of the big trees which grew thick just beyond the meadow. Arrows were striking the grass around him as the English archers tried long-distance shots. He struck the spurs into Sheila's flank again. "Come on, girl, come on!"

He took a hasty glance over his shoulder. The English had not left the highway. They were gathered in a little group, their leader shaking his fist angrily. The bowmen stood beside the cluster of men-at-arms, still sending their arrows arching into the air, trying to bring Hugh down with a lucky shot. But the range was too far. Hugh knew he was safe.

Finally he reached the edge of the forest and wiped the sweat from his forehead as he pulled Sheila up under the branches of a huge oak. "Whew! That was close!"

"Aye."

Hugh froze in his saddle as he heard the strange voice, the fingers of his right hand searching for the hilt of his sword. Turning cautiously, he could see, deep in the underbrush, a man on horseback sitting quietly, a bow in his hand and fingers on the string. But the stranger did not move.

Hugh found his voice at last. "Who are you, sir?"

The stranger beckoned. "Ride farther back into the trees, where we can be alone. I do not trust your friends on the Ayr road."

"No friends of mine. They are English."

The man with the bow, tall and lean in a green tunic very much like Hugh's, smiled slightly. "I know, lad. And when I see a stout young fellow running from them, I decide that he must be a friend to Scotland, and the Bruce."

"You are right, sir. I seek King Robert and his army."

The other put out his hand. "I am Jock Lockhart, a scout for the king, set to watch the highway. I'll take you to the camp at once. But how are you called?"

"Hugh Gordon, sir."

"Let's get started. The English over there just might decide to follow us."

Hours later, Jock Lockhart still led the way through the forest of Glen Trool, with Hugh close behind. They traveled single file on the narrow path which led through birch and ash and oak trees. Sheila kept on the heels of Lockhart's shaggy Galloway pony, as the shadows lengthened.

The trail led into high country which Hugh had never seen. Jock turned in his saddle and looked back. "The king is safe in these hills, Hugh Gordon, but he cannot stay hid forever. Sooner or later he must fight—and win— a battle against the English."

"Aye." Hugh's hand dropped to his sword hilt. "The sooner the better."

The other looked at him curiously. "I was like that

once, young and eager for swordplay. But I have seen too much of it. I'd rather be home at Ellerslie, hunting deer."

"And yet you fight?"

"Yes, I fight. Until we have freed Scotland from the invader. Until the king is on his throne again."

It was pitch dark when they started to ascend the rocky heights which overlooked Loch Doon. There was no sound now, except the clatter of hoofs on the granite trail. Once in a while a night bird called, then an unbroken stillness.

"We're almost there, lad," Jock said cheerfully. "Loch Doon is below. In a few minutes we'll reach the ridge where the Scots army is stationed."

"Let's hurry."

"Patience, young Gordon. We will not fight the English tonight. Our Scots need a good sleep."

The trail turned upward again. High through a rocky pass, it led into a wide meadow where campfires blazed in a huge semicircle around a rude farmhouse. There was a quiet hum of voices from Scots busy cooking or cleaning their weapons.

A sentinel challenged, and Jock Lockhart answered as they dismounted at a fire nearby. Lockhart walked into the firelight, and was greeted heartily by a big man with black, unruly hair. He looked critically at Hugh. "Who's the lad?"

"This is Hugh Gordon, men. He's come to join us."

The big man clapped Hugh on the shoulder. "Thou'rt but a boy. Can you use the sword you carry, young sir?"

"I will use it tomorrow. The king told me to come when I was ready, and I am here. Can I see him tonight, sir?"

"The king! He cannot be disturbed tonight, Hugh Gordon. Morning is soon enough. But make yourself at home. I'm sorry our oatcakes are cold, Jock."

"No matter," Jock said carelessly. "Cold food tonight, hot work tomorrow."

Next morning, Jock Lockhart took Hugh to the farm-house which was the king's headquarters. As they walked toward the building, Hugh looked curiously at the troops preparing breakfast. Not more than eight hundred here, he decided. Not a very big army with which to save Scotland. Not too many more than the number Gideon had.

Here and there, Hugh noticed kilted Highlanders from the mountains to the north, some with the deadly Loch-aber ax, others carrying the great two-handed claymore. Close to the farmhouse stood men-at-arms, followers of the various knights who fought for the king. They talked and laughed easily among themselves, leaning on their long lances or curbing their chargers. Hugh envied them. It would be wonderful to ride into battle in the company of such warriors.

As they reached headquarters, a tall, stern-faced man in black armor barred the door. When he recognized Jock, his face softened. " 'Tis good to see you again, Lockhart. Did you find any English on the Ayr road?"

"Just a dozen archers and men-at-arms who were chasing my friend here. Sir James Douglas, this is Hugh Gordon of Glenbirnie. He has come to fight for Scotland."

"And welcome you are, Hugh Gordon." Douglas extended his hand cordially. "We need all the men we can find."

"Thank you, Sir James."

"My friend wants to see the king for a minute," Jock said.

"A minute! Half a minute perhaps!" Sir James Douglas eyed Hugh sternly. "Wait here."

Sir James disappeared inside the farmhouse. Hugh felt beads of sweat on his forehead. He was not sure King

Robert remembered the boy who had shared his adventure in the forest of Glen Trool months ago. Hugh decided that he might possibly be thrown out of the Bruce's camp as a spy.

Before he could tell Jock of his misgivings, the tall man in black armor reappeared. "Enter, Hugh Gordon, but be hasty. We move against the English in an hour."

Hugh's heart was beating fast as he entered the room and fell on one knee before the well-remembered figure of Robert Bruce. "Sire, I have come to fight for you," he said looking directly at the king.

"Rise, young man." The tall monarch looked closely at his visitor. "I seem to know you," he said doubtfully.

"I am the boy with the gifted eyes, sire. A year ago, in the forest of Glen Trool, you were set upon by three men. I was there. You told me to return home and come back when I was older and stronger."

"To be sure." King Robert was smiling now. "You have grown so tall and heavy I did not recognize you. The name is Hugh Gordon of Glenbirnie, at least that is what Sir James Douglas called you."

"Yes, sire."

"Your father, as I recall it, is an old man, living at Glenbirnie. He knows you have sought me out?"

"Oh, yes. My father begged me to join you. For my own protection."

"What do you mean, lad? No army is a safe place—for a man who wants to save his skin!"

"It's not that, sire. A cousin of mine, a false Scot named Alan Gordon, has threatened to betray me to the English. To protect me, my father gave Glenbirnie to him, retaining only a life interest. And he urged me to join your army."

"We will talk of this later. This morning we will fight

an English force moving toward us up the valley of the Cree. Hast thou a horse, lad?"

"Yes, sire."

"Keep near me, Hugh Gordon. I remember those sharp eyes of yours and may have need of them."

"I shall be close behind you, sire."

Half an hour later, the little Scots force moved in files of four down a narrow path which led to the rocky ridge overlooking the blue waters of Loch Doon. As the army reached the location chosen for battle, the Scots spread out, concealing themselves in clumps of birch and pine.

Hugh, interested in the ambush being prepared for the English, tied Sheila to a tree and walked to the edge of the rocky height up which the English had to march if they expected to locate Robert Bruce. Standing on the ridge, he could see directly down into the glen of Trool which widened out into the broad stretch of ground along the Cree River.

Looking into the distance, Hugh could make out long lines of men approaching the lake. It was the English army, moving boldly to meet the Scots in the rocky country above Loch Doon.

"Hugh Gordon!" Hugh recognized the king's voice and ran forward immediately.

"Tell me, lad, what see you down the valley of the Cree? How many men do the English muster?"

Shading his eyes against the sharp morning sunlight, Hugh peered into the distance. "I see men advancing, sire, all on foot. Some of them are archers. Others are men-at-arms, walking beside the bowmen." He hesitated. "About fifteen hundred men, I would say."

"There is a lot of boggy ground down there," Sir James Douglas said. "That is why the knights have dismounted."

He turned to Hugh. "You have eyes like an eagle, young sir. I can see nothing at this distance."

As the English marched closer, every man in Bruce's army could distinguish the figures of the bowmen and men-at-arms moving with military precision up the glen. Hugh could feel his heart beating faster. He had not yet struck a blow in battle, and he could not keep from feeling uneasy. Those English closing in were professional soldiers, and he was a raw country boy.

Hugh and the other Scots had long ago blended with the landscape. Even King Robert was lying on the ground behind a bush, eyes intent on the enemy.

Hugh could see the English marching around the head of the loch. Now and then one would look up, searching the high ridge for signs of the enemy, but not a single Scots head showed above the foliage.

As the English van circled the loch and started its climb up the rocky path leading to the Scottish ambush, Hugh felt his arms grow tense. A dozen yards away, Jock Lockhart crouched, eyes fixed on the troops below. Beyond him Sir James Douglas stood behind a huge oak tree, leaning on his sword. Slightly to the rear, Scots archers quietly fitted arrows to their bows.

The English scouts were now less than fifty yards from the top of the ridge. Now and then they halted, looking upward at the trees and brush, then continued their cautious advance.

The English were now only a few yards away from Hugh. His blood chilled as he heard a high keening screech from a Highlander in a red kilt who leaped onto the shoulders of an English man-at-arms toiling up the path. The two men rolled off the trail and down to the shore of the loch, the Highlander stabbing as he fell.

A wild yell came from the Scots posted around Hugh.

As the bowmen poured a galling fire of arrows on the English, Hugh pulled his bonnet low and scrambled down to the path, sword in hand. The invaders, recovering from their surprise, began to fight fiercely.

Hugh staggered as his foot slipped on a large boulder. Not more than ten feet away, a tall Englishman in mail rushed at him. Hugh struck aside the first stroke of his opponent's sword, then ducked back. The Englishman advanced again, cutting and thrusting. Hugh stabbed at him, catching the return stroke on the edge of a shield he had borrowed from a wounded Scot.

Up and down the path the duel raged, neither Hugh nor the Englishman paying any attention to the general fighting. The Scots had begun to drive back the enemy, but Hugh was too busy to look. It was all he could do to save himself.

As the Englishman beat Hugh to his knees with a vicious cut, a Highlander leaped down on the back of the man-at-arms, dirk in hand. The man in armor shook him off and advanced again on Hugh, who struck hard, aiming at the Englishman's head. The blade struck the nosepiece of the helmet and bounced off.

Before Hugh could strike again, the Englishman swung his long sword. The stroke went home, denting Hugh's steel bonnet, knocking him unconscious to the ground.

This Land Is Ours

As he came back to his senses, Hugh felt a roaring in his ears, as though he had been engulfed in black waters and had barely been able to fight his way to the surface. He lay flat on the ground, with a Highlander's plaid rolled up under his head.

Jock Lockhart bent over him. "By Saint Andrew, lad, your head is made of iron. If I had had a clout like that, I'd be dead!"

A kilted Highlander knelt beside Lockhart, grinning companionably and talking so rapidly in Gaelic that Hugh could not follow him.

"You're using his plaid as a pillow," Jock explained. "Our friend here saved you from the Englishman. Hit him with a Lochaber ax."

"Did we win, Jock?"

"There's nothing left of the English force, except a few prisoners. Be quiet now. You have had a nasty knock, and the king's doctor told me not to move you."

Hugh closed his eyes. The ground was hard, but he felt good. At least he was alive. His head was splitting, as though he had been poleaxed like a Galloway steer, but he knew he had been lucky. Better men than Hugh Gordon, veterans of many battles, had died there by the loch.

For weeks, he stayed in bed by a campfire in the Scottish camp, at times so weak he could scarcely lift his head. Finally he got to his feet again and wandered through the meadow, his movements listless and his feet leaden. He felt as though all the energy had been drained from his body.

Hugh's long-drawn-out illness worried him. The Scots were attacking the English constantly from their base in the hills, conducting sharp hit-and-run raids, surprise attacks which shattered the morale of the enemy. But he, Hugh Gordon, was not a member of these raiding parties. No, he was left behind in camp. He felt strangely useless.

Jock Lockhart came looking for him one afternoon. "We're wanted by the king, Hugh. At once."

Entering headquarters, they found the king lying on a couch. He looked tired, his face drawn and pale, but he greeted both warmly. "Hugh Gordon, I am happy that your wound is no worse, but I feel you need a long rest. Think you Alan Gordon would find out, if you returned to Glenbirnie?"

"I do not know, sire." Hugh's face mirrored his disappointment. "I had hoped that you would need me here."

King Robert sighed. "I do need you. But I am going into North Scotland soon, to Aberdeen, because I am tired

and bone weary. My thought is that you can join me in
the fall. But you should rest at Glenbirnie for a few
months."

"Thank you, sire." Hugh felt enormously relieved.
King Robert was not trying to get rid of him. The Bruce
needed him and wanted him!

The king smiled. "It is settled, then. Lockhart, I want
you to ride to Glenbirnie with our young friend. Return
quickly, because we leave at once for the north. You may
go now. I wish a word in private with Hugh."

As Lockhart left the room, the king lay back on the
couch as if exhausted. "Come closer, young Gordon. I
have something to tell you. I am not a well man. Years of
flight and hunger have taken their toll. I have been like a
fox running just a few yards ahead of the hounds. In
Aberdeen I will be among friends. I will not have to run.
You understand?"

"Yes, sire."

"Good. Stay hidden safely from Alan Gordon. When
the first bite of the frost fills the air, mount and ride for
Dundee. You saw me crowned at Scone. Dundee is close
by, on the Firth of Forth."

"I can find it, sire."

"At Dundee you will go to a tavern called the Red
Lion Inn and look for one Angus Maclean. He will be
the biggest man you have ever seen, I think, a black
Highlander with a fist like iron and a crafty brain, for one
without book learning. Angus pretends to be a cattle
drover, but he is a spy for his king. Angus Maclean is my
ears in North Scotland. I hope that you in time will be
my eyes, Hugh Gordon."

"If Your Highness wishes it."

"I do wish it. You know, Hugh, there are many ways to
serve our poor country. Some men die for Scotland on

the field of battle. But you and Angus Maclean can use your wits for Scotland in the camp of the enemy. There is a risk, of course. It could go hard with you, if caught. My friend Black Angus takes that risk at the Red Lion and elsewhere, he goes boldly in among the English and listens, and the information he picks up comes back to me. I will see him at Aberdeen. Shall I tell him to expect you at Dundee, Hugh?"

"I shall be at the Red Lion on time, sire, unless I am in an English dungeon."

"Good. Be careful, lad. For you I have great hopes. In this hour of Scotland's need, we must work and fight to drive the English invader from our country. This is our land, Hugh, and though we be a small nation, we are entitled to our freedom. Good-by and Godspeed."

Hugh rose to go. "God keep you, sire."

He went into the outer hall where Jock Lockhart was waiting. "Everything's ready, Hugh. I've saddled Sheila and packed your gear. Let's be off."

That night they camped close to the Ayr highway under a great oak tree. Hugh made a fire, over which Jock Lockhart fried slices of mutton on his round black iron skillet. They ate quickly, then slept until dawn beside their grazing horses.

Next morning, they rode rapidly until they came to the crossroad which led to Glenbirnie. They approached the castle cautiously just before noon. If Cousin Alan was visiting the place there might be trouble, Hugh decided. He was glad Jock Lockhart was along.

Jock looked appreciatively at the stout walls of the keep, as they rode beside Loch Urr. "A man could hold off a small army here, Hugh." He eyed his companion thoughtfully. "Are't tired, lad? You're almost home now."

They drew rein in the courtyard and dismounted. "I'm

a bit tired, Jock, but all right. I need a good night's sleep."

"You need a good month's sleep," Jock retorted. "See that you get it."

The door of the keep opened, and Thomas Dickson came down to meet the riders, his blue eyes alight. "Welcome home, young sir. But what brings you here?"

"A broken head," Jock Lockhart said.

Hugh shook hands with Old Thomas. "I was wounded at the Battle of Loch Trool. The king sent me home, with my good friend Jock Lockhart. How is my father?"

"Not well, but he will be happy to see you."

"Take care of Sheila and Jock's horse, Thomas, will you? I want you to meet my father, Jock. He's a proud man and a good man."

That night Gavin Gordon's eyes sparkled as Hugh told him of his adventures with King Robert. The elder Gordon could not hear enough of the battle. "We beat them, lads, and it is only the beginning, eh, Lockhart? Scotland will be free again."

"Aye, Gordon," Jock said. "And your lad Hugh will play his part. He already has."

As Jock Lockhart mounted to ride away the following morning, Hugh felt lonesome and depressed. "I wish I were going with you, to the north."

"Stay and rest, Hugh. And, while you're enjoying life here, think of me on some lonely moor, hungry and cold, trying to hide from the English."

Jock laughed and shook hands, then trotted away.

Hugh was not so sure he would have a quiet summer. His father had said that Cousin Alan rarely visited the castle, but Hugh knew he would have to be careful. It was common knowledge at Douglaston that he had been wounded at Glen Trool. Some peasant might talk.

After Jock had ridden out of sight, Hugh walked over

to the stables under the keep while Jamie frisked and leaped around him as though he had never left. Red Rufus whinnied and thrust his muzzle into the crook of Hugh's arm.

Farther down the stable stood Sheila, her dark eyes watching Hugh. He walked over and patted her flank, just as Thomas Dickson opened the door and leaned a hay fork against the side of the stall.

"Thomas," Hugh said, "you remember that hut on the other side of the lake, where we used to rest after hunting?"

"Aye. 'Tis a little the worse for wear, but the roof can be fixed with fresh pine bows to keep out the rain."

"Good. I'm going to live there this summer, Thomas. If my cousin Alan pays Glenbirnie a visit, my father can truthfully say that I came to the castle here at one time, but have been gone for weeks."

"A good idea, lad. I can watch the keep here—and Alan Gordon." Bitterness crept into the old man's voice. "At the first sign of trouble, I'll steal away in the night and warn you."

That summer went quickly for Hugh Gordon, who stayed close to the hut and loafed in the sun. He could feel the strength flowing back into his body. Each day he exercised with light sword and shield, and he soon felt stronger.

Once a week, Old Thomas came with word that all was well at the castle. "Your father is feeble, young sir, but he thanks God and the saints that you are recovering. And that Alan Gordon does not darken his door. You feel much better, eh? I can tell."

"Yes, Thomas, I do." Hugh touched his head. "For weeks, I suffered from dizziness and headache. But I am strong again. Before long, I will take my bow and flush some game."

"I will go with thee, lad. But do not practice swordplay too soon. I received a blow like yours years ago. Months passed before I felt sound and whole again."

Hugh went grouse hunting the next day. Later that week, Thomas Dickson joined him, and the two of them killed enough game to keep the larder of the castle full for a long time.

Now and then, Hugh would ride Sheila down to Glenbirnie, under cover of darkness, and the two Gordons would have a joyous reunion. At such times Gavin Gordon could not long keep his eyes from the figure of his son, grown so strong and rugged.

"Thou art very much like my father, Hugh," the elder Gordon said one night as they sat in the great hall. "Sir Alexander Gordon, your grandfather, was a bold man and a strong one. Belike you will be the same."

"I hope so, sir, for your sake."

Gavin Gordon shook his head. "My boy, I am thinking of you and your future. I am about done for, but you will be a great man some day, if Robert Bruce regains his throne." The elder Gordon's head fell against the back of the great oak chair, and he slept, breathing heavily.

September was cooler, so much so that Hugh slept with a blanket over him. He was almost himself again and restless. His appetite was immense. He could not get enough of his own cooking, oatcakes baked on a flat skillet, grouse, venison, with now and then potatoes and eggs brought from the castle.

Once more he started to practice with the sword under the watchful eye of Thomas Dickson. First, he carefully whittled a small oak tree into a post six feet high. Then he walked around it, cutting and slashing for an hour at a time. Then, sweaty and tired, he would lie down and sleep for an hour.

Old Thomas was complimentary. "You are supple and strong, Hugh Gordon. It is because you are older, lad. What a pity that you cannot practice with the lance in the tiltyard, as you used to do! Every gentleman should learn how to fight on horseback against his equals."

"I'm not so sure of that, Thomas. At Glen Trool, the English dismounted their men-at-arms, to fight against us. Both Scots and English, knights, spearmen and archers battled hand to hand, on the ground. I was wounded, but if I had been on horseback, I might have been hurt worse."

"The knight with the lance and sword will always win wars, young sir. Us common men cannot stand up to the nobility."

"If to fight on foot is to be common, I am common," Hugh said cheerfully. "Our country is a land of peasants, Thomas. It is hill and glen and moor and morass. In Scotland, the English knight will always fight at a disadvantage."

"You are not common," Old Thomas said emphatically. "You are Gordon of Glenbirnie."

"So be it. Watch my sword work once more. See if I strike too high."

When the first cold wind blew in from the north, bringing a foretaste of winter, Hugh moved back to the castle. He had heard practically nothing of King Robert's army. It had seemed to disappear into the wilds of Aberdeen.

The English were everywhere in Scotland, garrisoning the big castles and towns. Their men-at-arms and archers marched arrogantly along the highroads. Along the edge of the Highlands Scots made sudden sorties against the invader, then fled rapidly into the hills. But there was no

organized resistance. Hugh feared it was because the
king was not only a hunted man but a sick man. Restlessly
he bided his time against departure.

A cold mist blew down on Glenbirnie the day Hugh
started for Dundee. He wore his coat of mail under his
tunic, as usual, and a long woolen plaid which fell from
his shoulder and partially concealed his sword.

After bidding his father and the Dicksons good-by, he
rode Sheila up the glen which led to the Ayr road. Reaching that highway, Hugh looked back in the direction of
Dumfries before heading north. He could see no sign
of English soldiers, but his sharp eyes caught sight of
two riders.

There was something familiar about the hunched
shoulders of the man in front. Hugh looked again. It was
Alan Gordon!

"Well," Hugh muttered to himself, "I have left Glenbirnie just in time." He whirled and set spurs to Sheila.
As she dashed north, he turned in his saddle and shook
his fist defiantly at the oncoming horseman. A childish
gesture, he thought afterward, but a very human one.

The mist stung his face on the long miles to Ayr, as
the wind blew in from the north. He wrapped himself
closer in the plaid and rode on. Reaching Ayr, he circled
to the east of the town whose castle had a strong English
garrison.

Many miles later, on the Glasgow road, he stopped at
a peasant's hut for food. He did not dare visit the taverns
in the small towns, because English men-at-arms were
everywhere, as were Scots traitors who would hasten to
betray him. Only in the rude homes of the common people
could he depend on fidelity and kindliness.

The country grew hillier as he skirted Glasgow and
took the highroad toward Stirling, his immediate destina-

tion. But he did not dare cross the Forth River at Stirling, for the bridge would be watched carefully by English guards.

Cutting to the west of the town, he reached the Forth, where he found a ferry which took him across. Then he headed back for Stirling, bone weary and haggard, worn out by the mist and the rain. Once he arrived in town, he promised himself, he would go to an inn, get a decent night's sleep and be off for Perth in the early morning.

It was late afternoon before Hugh reached the town and looked with awe at the castle which crowned a high hill. The frame-and-stone houses of the burghers were clustered together beneath the high keep where the flag with the three English lions fluttered in the breeze.

Stirling was the biggest town Hugh had ever seen, and his wide eyes took in every sight as Sheila walked slowly down the cobblestoned streets lined with shops. He was enjoying himself, as he always did when visiting a strange place.

Now and then, Sheila would be crowded out of the middle of the street by marching English archers on their way to the castle on the hill. Hugh would pull the mare quickly to one side. He was glad his father had insisted that he dress like a peasant instead of a knight. None of the bowmen swaggering by could know that there was a coat of mail under his tunic.

Near the center of the town, Hugh came to an inn. Cautiously he sat his horse for half an hour, watching people go in and out the front door of the tavern. Satisfied no English soldiers were there, he guided Sheila through the arched gateway to the stables at the rear. After a stableboy had led the mare to a stall, he squared his shoulders and walked boldly into the inn.

The Trap

Hugh slept late that morning. As he woke slowly and stretched, he realized how lucky he'd been. The night before, he had dined boldly in the big room downstairs. Nothing had happened. Apparently the inn was not patronized by the English in Stirling.

He listened to the sleet tapping against the window and wished he were making this trip in summer, under smiling skies. But he remembered that cold weather kept the Englishman close to his fire. A lone Scot, riding for the Bruce, had less chance of detection and arrest in winter.

He dressed, then walked downstairs for a hot breakfast and went to the stables where he found Sheila already saddled. Tossing the hostler a silver piece, he mounted and rode down the cobbled street, heading north.

Hugh hoped to make Perth that night, but he knew the sleet would slow him down. Reaching the edge of the town, he followed a road which wound through the Ochil hills. He was not familiar with the territory but expected to strike the Earn River by noon.

Three hours brought him to the stream, where he stopped in the shelter of a peasant's barn for a scanty meal of cold oatcakes and cheese. Then he was off again, riding down the river road toward Perth.

Sheila plodded patiently through the weather, her head bowed as the sleet came slanting down. Hugh wrapped his woolen plaid around his shoulders, keeping a sharp eye out for wandering English horsemen. But none were about, preferring comfort to adventure on the highroad.

By late afternoon Hugh had reached the point where the Earn joins the Tay River, rolling down from the Highlands. The road veered sharply to the left and Sheila slowed her pace. Hugh brushed the sleet from the mare's ears. "A little farther, Sheila, and we'll both eat and be warm."

An hour later he guided the mare down the rough cobblestones on the main street of Perth to the two-story wood and stone Black Boar Inn. Behind the building he could see a courtyard which ran far to the rear of the inn and stables. This, Hugh noted, was an area which ran close to the Tay. Enclosed as it was with a big wooden fence, it might be a hard place to leave in a hurry.

He hesitated, sitting uneasily in his saddle. Sheila pawed impatiently, then turned and nipped at his boot. Hugh knew he was taking a risk, but after all, he wasn't a boy, hunting rabbits. He was almost a man, and a trusted follower of King Robert.

He slapped Sheila's flank sharply with the reins and rode into the dimly lighted courtyard where a sleepy stableboy came forward and held the mare while he dismounted. "Here's a silver piece, lad. Give the horse a good rubdown and feed her well."

Stiff with cold, he walked slowly to the rear of the courtyard. Just outside the stable wall he could hear the rush of the Tay River. He followed the row of stalls until he reached a door at the back of the horse barn. Cautiously he opened it and looked out. He had been right. The river was only a few yards away.

On his way back to the Black Boar he examined the courtyard again. There was only one entrance into the enclosure, the arched gate by the inn. A man could very well be trapped here unless he wished to swim the river.

Arranging his plaid to conceal the sword in his belt, Hugh went into the public room and was relieved to see none of the few customers present wore the green of the English archers or the mail shirt of the Norman men-at-arms. There were only elderly burghers of the town, drinking their mulled wine and gossiping quietly in small groups.

When Hugh asked for a room the red-faced innkeeper gave him a sharp glance. "Pay in advance, young sir."

Hugh paid gladly and took a table in the corner of the room where he could eat his mutton pie in peace. Food made him feel better and the warmth of the room had driven away the memory of his long, cold ride. He looked around at his neighbors. Only one man seemed to notice him.

The stranger was a Highlander wearing a plaid which Hugh could not identify, a kilt and tunic with a dirk stuck in one woolen stocking.

Thoughtfully Hugh applied himself to his supper. Some

of the clans, he knew, were friendly to the English. This man might be a MacDougall of Lorn and an enemy of the Bruce.

Suddenly the Highlander rose and walked to Hugh's table, speaking with a pronounced accent. "Young sir, we have met before?"

"I think not. I am from Galloway."

"Galloway!" The stranger's eyes became curiously intent. "That is the home of the king, is it not?"

Hugh sensed the play on words. If he referred to the Bruce as King Robert, he would be identifying himself as a king's man. This Highlander might well be a spy for the English. Hugh chose his words carefully. "Galloway is, indeed, the home of the Earl of Carrick, whom many Scots call king. Now, if you will excuse me, I am tired from a long ride."

Hugh pushed back the bench and walked slowly across the room. Not until he was halfway up the stairs did he look back. The tavern keeper and the Highlander had their heads together, talking. About what, he could only guess. The two men, of course, could be old friends. But their faces gave him a strange uneasiness.

Even in his room he could not rid himself of the feeling he was being watched. He stared out the window into the black night. A birch tree fingered the frosty window-panes with wet branches. Carefully he swung the casement window out and examined the bare limbs. They would hold his weight if he had to reach the ground in a hurry.

With the vague threat still haunting him, he tugged and hauled at a heavy oak chest until he had placed it in front of his door. He went to bed with the satisfaction of knowing any Englishman would have hard work breaking down the door to make an arrest. He stirred restlessly, trying to sleep in his coat of mail, but he knew that safety outweighed comfort in an emergency.

What wakened him before dawn he did not know. But some instinct told him to be on guard. Quietly he crept out of bed, buckled on his sword, and fitted his steel bonnet tightly over his head.

Still no sound came from the hall. Everything was quiet, too quiet. Through the birch branches outside the window he could see the stables where the dim light of a burning pine knot flickered just inside the door. Nothing moved. There was only the silence, punctuated by the drip, drip of the rain.

Then the stillness was shattered explosively by a heavy fist at the door of Hugh's room. "Open! Open in the name of King Edward!" He heard feet moving. Someone shoved at the door, moving the oak chest back several inches. "Open up, Scot! We would have words with thee!"

Noiselessly, Hugh ran to the window and eased himself over the sill, into the branches of the birch tree. Swiftly he slid down the trunk to the ground.

Running headlong through the darkness of early morning, he reached the stables, shaking the sleepy stableboy awake. "Quick, lad, my horse! Saddle the mare at once!"

The boy rubbed his eyes with a grimy fist and finally got to his feet. Impatiently Hugh rushed past him into Sheila's stall and put the saddle and blanket on her back. Then he backed her around and made for the front door.

He rode out of the stable into the glare of pine torches which lit up the courtyard. Blocking his escape through the archway beside the Black Boar Inn were a dozen English men-at-arms stolidly sitting their chargers. Beside the horsemen stood a small clump of archers, bows at the ready.

He was caught like a fox in his hole!

A tall man in armor walked a few steps forward, cupping his hands to his mouth. "Young Scot, you are our prisoner. Surrender or be killed!"

Hugh saw the archers bending their longbows in the light of the flaming torches. Suddenly he jerked hard on the black mare's rein. She wheeled as Hugh dug in the spurs and bolted back inside the stable door, while the English arrows rattled close.

There was a yell from the courtyard and the clatter of hoofs on the rough cobblestones. Hugh knew the men-at-arms were riding hard for the stable door. He was caught, unless he rode to the rear of the stable and spurred his horse out into the rain-swollen waters of the Tay!

He hesitated for a second, then turned Sheila to the left. As he opened the back door, he heard the harsh tramp of feet. The English began a methodical search of the stalls in the barn. He knew he could not delay a second longer. He must trust himself to the black waters of the river.

Again Hugh spurred Sheila, and the little mare sprang, trembling, out into the Tay. Horse and rider hit the water with a tremendous splash. As they went under, Hugh decided that no mountain stream in Galloway had ever had colder water.

The current was so swift it quickly swept Hugh and the mare downstream. Turning in his saddle, he could make out the dim figures of men crowded around the door he had just left, but the speed of the river was so great that no enemy archer had a chance to send a shaft after him.

If he could only swim the mare directly across the Tay to the opposite bank he could find the shallows and firm footing there. But he could see now that the river was too swollen for the little mare to make it. The water sucked at his waterlogged boots and heavy clothing. He could feel

Sheila battling the current, but tiring in the bitter-cold water.

Then he remembered a quiet pool he had seen on the Perth side a few miles down the stream. Here the current lessened in the shallows. He knew his only chance of survival was to guide Sheila into those shallows, climb up the bank and reach the stone bridge on the highway before the English tried to cut him off.

He pulled Sheila's rein sharply to the right and the mare responded, swimming slowly but surely as though she sensed safety ahead.

He had no way of knowing how far below Perth they had drifted. He strained his eyes to catch a glimpse of lights on shore, but there was only darkness as the water swirled around his legs aching with cold.

Frantically he clung to Sheila's neck. "Come on, Sheila lass, come on!"

Hugh struggled on, pointing the mare's head toward what he hoped was the bank of the river. It seemed forever before he felt Sheila's feet hit the shallows and stumble tiredly toward the shore.

The water was below his stirrups now. His teeth chattered as the icy wind hit his wet clothes. But twenty feet away he could make out the dim outline of trees.

With a final effort, Sheila pulled up the steep bank and stood blowing and trembling with exhaustion. Hugh dismounted stiffly, slapping his hands to start the circulation, whispering his thanks to the staunch little mare.

He knew he should stop and dry his soaking clothes and give Sheila a brisk rub, but comfort he could not afford. The English in Perth would be on his trail like hounds chasing a stag. He could lose no time in getting to Angus Maclean at Dundee.

Wearily he mounted and urged the mare across the meadow to the main road where he could see or hear no movement, no sign of pursuit from the English.

He knew he had a head start which he must not lose. Cautiously he rode onto the deserted highway and turned south. If he expected to reach the road to Dundee and cross that stone bridge over the Tay he could waste no time. Yet he did not have the heart to drive Sheila faster. She was spent and walked slowly, too slowly if English horsemen appeared.

As it became lighter, Hugh turned in his saddle and looked down the empty road. There were no pursuers. Perhaps they thought he had been drowned. Or perhaps they waited for him at the stone bridge, the only bridge across the Tay for many miles.

Riding became torture. Cold, sleepless, hungry and tired, he plodded on another five miles until the stone bridge loomed suddenly out of the mist of the morning. He half expected a challenge or a rain of arrows. But none came. There was no one at the bridge. With numb lips he offered a prayer to Saint Andrew. "Truly, I am fortunate above all other men. I thank you." He knew he was as exhausted as Sheila. If his life had depended on his sword arm, he could have struck not a single blow.

An hour later he was still riding miserably on beside the ever-widening Firth of Tay toward Dundee, which seemed a million miles away. Again and again he turned to look for English riders but none thundered down the lonely highway. Now and then he passed a lone traveler. The stranger would pull to one side of the road, Hugh to the other. They would eye each other suspiciously like two strange dogs. Then each would travel on.

The English have done that to Scotland, Hugh thought

bitterly. They have made every man wary of the other. King Edward I had set the Scots at each other's throats. His son, King Edward II, had continued that policy, wooing the great nobles, killing off ruthlessly those who would not swear allegiance. King Robert in the hands of the English would be as good as dead.

Sheila's gait was slower now. Hugh wheeled again in his saddle, his hawk's eyes piercing the distance. But there was still no sign of life on the road. Feeling the mare trembling, Hugh came to a quick decision. No matter what the risk, he would stop at a peasant's house and dry his clothes while the mare had at least an hour's rest and some food.

But the road wound through a lonely stretch of country. There were no huts, no sign of life. Finally, Hugh dismounted and led the tired horse whose head drooped, whose breath was shallow and labored.

Just before noon, he pulled rein in front of a stone cottage set well back from the Dundee road. Obviously, it was the home of a prosperous peasant, very probably a loyal Scot. With a numb fist Hugh knocked. There was no reply. The second time he beat on the door, a harsh voice answered, "Who are ye?"

Hugh shifted his hand to the hilt of his sword. "A Scot, and a weary traveler."

The door opened slowly. A tall, spare, redheaded man looked him up and down, his eyes missing nothing. "A Scot, eh, but what kind of Scot?"

Hugh took the plunge. "I am for King Robert."

"Why didn't ye say so? In with you, sir."

"As a matter of fact," Hugh said slowly, "the English are tracking me from Perth. I am Hugh Gordon of Glenbirnie."

"Put the mare in the barn out back, sir. There's hay and oats for her. Ye can stay here until the English ride past."

Hugh hesitated. "They might take it into their heads to search the house."

"Not likely. The rain will wash out all traces of your mare's hoofs."

As they walked to the barn, Hugh thanked the farmer for his hospitality. "I am cold and hungry but I would not bring death on this house. If the English find me here, it might well go hard with you."

"It's a chance my wife and I are willing to take, young sir." The peasant's face was set grimly. "The English killed my boy, and him no older than you."

Inside the cottage, the peasant introduced his wife, who was cooking a savory stew in a big pot hung over the fire which blazed in the middle of the room. The smell of mutton, onions and potatoes filled the air, making Hugh realize how hungry he was. He beckoned to his host. "I must get out of these clothes or freeze. Can you lend me hose and tunic while mine dry?"

The peasant led him into a rear room, where he peeled off his tunic and mail shirt, also the long, wet woolen hose which clung like ice to his thighs. The farmer gave him fresh clothes, and he was soon eating heartily in the main room, lingering over his oatcakes and mutton stew.

An hour later he rode away, revived and refreshed. As he waved good-by to the kindly couple who had befriended him, he felt like a new man. His clothes were dry, his stomach was full. Sheila, having been fed and rested, had regained some of her old-time spirit. The rain had stopped, and the sun was out.

Hugh felt at peace with the world as he jogged along toward Dundee, but his bump of caution caused him to turn around and look behind. Far to the rear, his keen eyes caught the glint of mail flashing in the sun. He looked again. There were men-at-arms riding two by two. His enemies were again on his trail, and their horses were undoubtedly fresh!

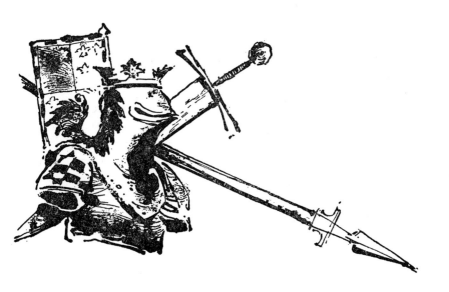

Shield of Snow

H ugh spurred Sheila suddenly and the mare
leaped forward. The English as yet were
far behind, but Hugh did not want them any closer. He
was not sure the men following were the same soldiers
who had tried to trap him at Perth, but if they were, certainly they would not give up the chase.

He looked down at Sheila galloping along steadily. She
had had rest and feed, but he knew that dip in the Tay
River had taken its toll. How long the mare's stout heart
and legs could hold out, he did not know. He wondered if
the men behind had noticed his increased speed. He
could not be sure but a quick look told him the English
were already narrowing the gap.

The wind was blowing from the north now, bringing stinging flakes of snow drifting over the road with the first touch of winter. Since Hugh did not know this country well he hoped he could reach Dundee before drifts made him lose his way.

But as the snow became heavier, Hugh realized that the storm was indeed a blessing. The English could no longer see him through the white curtain. His hopes rose. Behind a shield of snow he might well reach Dundee and shake off his pursuers.

However, the shield of snow worked both ways. He had no idea of how close the English were. He could have no warning until he heard the arrows sing around him.

On he plodded through the soft white curtain until caution made him pull Sheila up and dismount. Kneeling with his ear to the snow-covered ground, he could hear the muffled hoofbeats of many horses. He leaped back into the saddle and drove the tired mare on.

For a moment he panicked. Then his head cleared. He could not turn off the Dundee road to the right, for that way led to the firth with the open sea beyond. But he could rein Sheila to the left and ride up some glen, biding his time until the English passed. True, if he could not locate a peasant's hut or find his way back to the road, he might be half frozen by morning, but he knew it was a chance he had to take.

A long mile farther toward Dundee, he noticed a group of birches near the road, their leafless branches heavy with snow. He checked Sheila and looked hard at the ground between the trees. It was only a sheep track running north from the highway, but without hesitation he left the road. Unless he had underestimated the speed of the English, the snow would cover his tracks before they reached the birch grove and galloped on.

He gave Sheila her head and plowed straight into the storm sweeping in from the north. He knew he had escaped the English but whether he could escape freezing to death he wasn't sure. He was roaming through an unknown glen with no peasant hut to be found, no gleam of friendly light in the wilderness of wind and cold.

He leaned over Sheila's snow-encrusted neck and whispered words of encouragement to the mare as she picked her way carefully through the mounting drifts. His hands began to grow numb on the reins and his head reeled with thoughts of the Red Lion Inn at Dundee. He could see the big roaring fire in the great fireplace of the common room. He could almost taste the ale and hear the roaring laughter of Black Angus Maclean who waited for him even now in the warmth of a room which seemed so far away.

He tried to reconstruct in his mind a crude map he had once seen of this part of Scotland. As near as he could figure, the sheep track led through the Sidlaws, a range of hills parallel to the Firth of Tay and to Dundee. If that be true, he was riding farther and farther away from his destination.

The path rose higher into the hills and Sheila moved with bent head as though it hurt her to walk. Finally, Hugh dismounted and rubbed her nose gently. "Come on, lass, somewhere we'll find a shelter." He did not sound convincing, but it was obvious the mare had reached the limit of her endurance.

Hugh shook the snow from his bonnet. "Sheila, girl, I've given you a rough time, but I had to do it. It was the only way we could escape the English."

The mare nipped his sleeve and tossed her mane as though she would try to go on. Hugh looked over the vast white waste of the countryside and admitted what he had known all along. "King Robert, your Galloway lad has gotten himself lost."

Fear began to settle on him like a clammy fog. He wished he were back at Glenbirnie, a boy again with his father and old Thomas. He thought of Jamie, the dog that had so often romped with him in the snow.

He stopped a moment to rest and almost twisted a smile from his half-frozen face. What a lot of time he was wasting feeling sorry for poor Hugh Gordon! After all, he had wanted to wear a man's sword and fight a man's war. If he was lost in the Sidlaw hills, it was because he had been a little bit too cocksure for a boy of fifteen.

Having faced the fact that he had turned off the road of his own accord and would have to make the best of his predicament, he stamped his feet and struggled on, pulling Sheila behind him.

He did not know how far he had walked when he ran into a band of sheep huddled close together in a clump of oak trees. There was no trace of the shepherd, but Hugh knew he must be close by.

Some of the sheep moved away from him and Sheila, but most of the woolly animals were packed close, snugged together for warmth against the storm. Hugh started to walk into the band, then stopped. Best stay where he was, for the shepherd on a night like this would eventually circle the band to watch his flock and pick up any strays, whether they be sheep or Galloway men lost in the snow.

Fighting to keep awake, Hugh huddled close to Sheila, grateful for the warmth of the horse's body. With effort he kept moving his feet so the sodden boots and wet woolen hose would not freeze to his legs. Sheila, exhausted, turned her back to the wind and let her head droop while icy snow clung to her coat.

The sheep were quiet now and Hugh felt the stillness

of the boundless cover of white. Suddenly he heard a bark echo through the night. Then the sound was swept away by the wind, leaving him with no clue as to where it came from. But Hugh felt his hopes kindle. The sheep dog must be near his master. The sound couldn't be too far off.

Eagerly he peered through the darkness, trying to make out form or shape. Then a low throaty growl came from behind him. A small dog with a heavy coat of black and white fur sat in the snow only a few feet away watching Hugh's every move.

"Jamie! Jamie!" Hugh called. Well he knew it was not his own Border collie, but he hoped to make a friend. He knelt in the snow and called again to the dog, hoping he wouldn't bound away into the darkness. "Here, laddie, here. I know a dog just like you in Galloway. Come to me, laddie."

The sheep dog remained motionless, but his growls ceased. Then he stood up and moved forward by inches, watching Hugh suspiciously until he could sniff the strange outstretched fingers and hear a pleading "Good laddie, fine laddie."

Making his movements slow and sure, Hugh patted the little collie's coat, stroked its cold nose and scratched its ears, talking constantly without raising his voice. "It's a fine dog you are and I wish I could take you with me to Glenbirnie. How you and Jamie could romp together!"

The collie suddenly darted away, barking loudly. A few minutes later, a shadowy figure emerged from the snow and walked slowly toward Hugh, a flaming pine torch in his hand.

Hugh called loudly to the stranger. "Good e'en, friend. I take you for a kindly Scot."

"Aye. And you?"

Hugh decided to be frank. "I am Hugh Gordon of Glenbirnie, looking for the road to Dundee. I am on the business of King Robert."

The old shepherd came closer. "Welcome to these wild hills, Gordon of Glenbirnie. If thou'rt on an errand for the king, God bless thee."

"I am running from the English. They followed me from Perth, and I had to leave the main road down by the firth. Is there any way I can get to Dundee?"

"No stranger could reach Dundee a night like this. In this weather, you would freeze to death. Come with me to my small hut over the hill. My fare is poor, but any loyal Scot is welcome to it."

The man pushed his way through the mass of sheep, with Hugh and Sheila close behind. Hugh walked slowly, keeping his eye fixed on the blazing torch ahead. Bleating ewes climbed out of the way to make room for a soldier and his horse.

Suddenly the hut rose out of the storm, offering welcome shelter. There was no barn, and Hugh tied the mare to a log outside. Inside the only room, the shepherd built a fire of pine knots, then spread out on the floor his shepherd's plaid of brown and white checks.

"Rest ye, Gordon of Glenbirnie," he said. "The pot is on the fire, and the stew will soon be ready."

Once on the plaid, Hugh almost fell asleep but the smell of the stew revived him. His host took a mutton bone and threw it to the collie at the door. "The snow has almost stopped," he said, looking into the night. "You can start for Dundee in the morning, young sir."

Hugh slept heavily. When morning came, the old man woke him. After he had dressed and eaten, he stepped to the door, and saw the snow had stopped and the sun was out. Sheila stood, stamping her hoofs, tossing her head, as if ready to depart. He rubbed the mare's smooth muzzle. "We'll be in Dundee soon, lass, and you'll eat oats again."

He washed his face in the snow and entered the hut. The shepherd was baking bannocks which he divided into two portions, giving most of it to Hugh. "Thou'rt young, lad, and need something to sustain thee."

Hugh was touched by the old man's kindliness. "I thank you. When I see King Robert, I'll tell him how many friends he has in Scotland."

"Tell the king that the common people love him. Tell him that, Gordon of Glenbirnie."

"That I will." Hugh stood up, wishing he could leave a gold piece in the shepherd's hut, knowing he dare not for fear of offending. Instead he buckled on his sword and walked to the door, giving the sheep dog's ears a friendly tug. "Good-by, old man. God be with thee."

He passed the oak grove where he had found the sheep during the snowstorm and galloped through the low range of hills below the Sidlaws where he had wandered so hopelessly the night before. By noon he had sighted the Dundee highway with the Firth of Tay beyond.

Hugh patted Sheila's flank in triumph. He was on his way, heading for the town where Black Angus Maclean waited at the Red Lion Inn. As he approached the outskirts of Dundee he became more confident. He had met no travelers on the road except wagoners and solitary horsemen. He had seen no English men-at-arms.

Yet, remembering his brashness of two nights before, he slowed Sheila to a walk as he wound through the narrow, twisting streets of the old seaport town. He reasoned that the Red Lion Inn would not be on the main square. It would be a second-best tavern, a quiet little place on some side street, where a spy for King Robert, like Black Angus, would be little noticed.

Cautiously, Hugh did not ask, but rode the streets until he found the long rambling building with a faded Red Lion facing the world proudly over the entrance from the cobblestone street.

He wished for a moment he had Jock Lockhart at his side, but one look at Sheila, tired and hungry, gave him the courage he needed. Boldly he rode into the courtyard and threw the reins to a stableboy, casually as Lockhart himself would have done. "Here's a silver piece, lad. Rub down the mare and give her oats. Be not niggardly."

"Aye, sir."

Then Hugh walked slowly into the Red Lion serving room where a cheerful fire blazed on the hearth and cast inviting warmth over the oak tables and benches. Seeing few customers in the late afternoon shadows, Hugh sauntered across the public room and paid for a night's lodging.

The innkeeper eyed him sharply but asked no questions. Hugh began to feel more sure of himself. "I am expecting to meet a friend here. Has one asked for me?"

The tavern keeper seemed indifferent. "None that I remember. Men come and men go at the Red Lion, young sir. It's all the same to me."

To Hugh, that statement could mean anything—enemy or friend. But he had to chance it. "Belike you've seen my friend. He would be big and dark. A Highlander."

The innkeeper shrugged. "Many of the kilted men come down from the hills. What is his name?"

Hugh hesitated. "Angus Maclean."

The man shook his head. "I know him not."

As he walked away, Hugh tried to hide his disappointment. He had been so sure Black Angus would be there to meet him, but he realized that the king's spy had a great deal of work to do.

He sank into an oak seat, and saw the innkeeper's light

blue eyes fixed on him in a speculative stare. It was not an unfriendly glance, but a thoughtful one which made Hugh vaguely uneasy.

The owner of the place talked like a Scot. He looked like a Scot. But he might very well be, secretly, a friend of England. He remembered the tavern keeper at Perth who had sold him out to the English. This man might be loyal, or he could be greedy, willing to pass on information to the enemy for a handful of gold.

After supper Hugh sat around watching the customers, then decided to get some sleep. As he opened the door of his room on the second floor, he heard a girl's soft voice with a note of urgency in it. "By your leave, master, by your leave! I would talk with thee."

His eyes at last located a small dark girl in the dress of a serving-woman.

"What do ye want, lassie?" Hugh asked mildly.

"I heard you ask the innkeeper about Angus Maclean, sir."

Hugh was suddenly interested. "You know him?"

"Aye, and a very fine man he is too. A true Scot."

"So he is a Scot, and you are a Scot, lassie, and so am I." Hugh hesitated a second, then went on. "God save King Robert."

"Amen, sir." The girl kissed his hand. "I am a serving-maid at the Red Lion. The former owner was a loyal Scot, a friend of Black Angus. But this one—I am not so sure. He loves gold too well. I think he would sell out to the English."

"I shall be careful, lass," Hugh said. "Where is Angus Maclean now?"

"I know not, sir. But this I do know, Black Angus will return on the morrow."

"Good." Hugh slipped a gold piece into the girl's hand

in spite of her protest. "I owe thee thanks, lass. Say no more about it."

"I must warn you, sir. The English come here often. They do not know who Angus Maclean is. They think him a Highland drover, big and slow and slightly stupid. But he is canny, like the red fox. So far he has given the English the slip."

"I shall watch for the English and for Black Angus. If you hear the innkeeper talking about me to anyone, come quickly and knock on the door three times. The English want me as they do Angus Maclean."

"I will remember, sir. Do you know Black Angus?"

"I have never seen him, lass."

"Tomorrow I will point him out to you if he comes. Good night, sir."

The Red Lion

Hugh awoke the next morning feeling alive and alert. He had slept without worry or fear, trusting that the little maid would be quick to warn him of any treachery.

As he lay in bed watching the sunshine pour through the window, he stretched and yawned, feeling the first faint stirrings of hunger. He rose and dressed rapidly, pulling the tunic and hose on over the linked shirt of armor, and buckling on the sword which had by now become second nature to him.

He walked casually down the stairs and looked around for the serving girl, but the dark-haired little maid was not to be seen. She must be back in the kitchen, he thought, as he found a table in the corner, ready and eager for breakfast.

Just then, a door in front of him swung open and the serving girl entered carrying a heavy tray. She nodded as she passed with a whispered "I'll see you soon, sir."

In a few moments she was back with a correct "What will ye have to eat now, sir?" Then she lowered her voice. "The man you seek is in this room. I'll point him out when you have eaten."

"Thank you kindly," Hugh said, and ordered loudly. "Bring me a tankard of mulled wine, some eggs and wheaten bread."

When the girl had disappeared into the kitchen, Hugh looked around the room again. There was only one customer who might be Angus Maclean. All he could see of the man was a head of black hair, close cropped, surmounting enormous shoulders.

Although the dark-haired man did not turn around, Hugh was certain it was Black Angus. He knew it would be wiser to pretend not to notice the Highlander so he concentrated on the eggs and bread the girl brought him while she stood by, watching. "A fine meal, lass," he said. "Now I would see Angus Maclean. Tell me, is he not sitting halfway down the hall on this side?"

"Aye, sir. That is the one you seek."

"Tell me, is there any man near him? I would not be overheard."

The girl shook her head. "No one is near his table."

Hugh rose and walked with no show of purpose toward the big Highlander. As he neared the table, Black Angus turned slowly and looked with seeming indifference when Hugh paused at his table.

"Can I do aught for you, sir?"

Now that his quest was ended, Hugh wasn't quite sure what he should say. "If you are the man I think you are, I'd like a minute of your time."

"Time's cheap, young sir. Draw up a chair."

Hugh sat down and came to the point. "I am Hugh Gordon of Glenbirnie, sir. We have a friend in common—Robert Bruce."

Angus Maclean squinted shrewdly at Hugh. "Many an Englishman has tried that ruse. How do I know you follow the Bruce?"

"I fought with the king at Glen Trool. I am to join him in the North, if you will take me there."

Angus looked hard at Hugh. "You seem frank enough, but these are hard times in Scotland. Who do you mistake me for?"

"There is no mistake. You are Angus Maclean. His Highness told me last spring when I went home wounded that I was to report to you at the Red Lion Inn as soon as I could travel. I am here."

Maclean eyed the boy in silence for a while. Gradually, his air of reserve melted, but he was still watchful. "You cannot blame me, in my business, for being careful, young sir. You are a Gordon, of a famous clan and name, but there have also been Gordons loyal to England instead of to King Robert. I am not trying to be offensive, ye understand."

The man lifted his huge bulk from the chair. "Let us go for a stroll, lad. I have something in mind."

Hugh walked along to the door of the inn with Angus and blinked at the sun on the cobblestone street. The Highlander peeked into the distance, then straightened his heavy shoulders. "Young man, this is off the main square. Yonder, three blocks away, stands the city hall. Beside the city hall is the guild hall, built by the master craftsmen of the town. Tell me, young sir, what is the Latin inscription over that entrance?"

For a moment Hugh could not understand what Angus

was doing. Then he realized that this was the final test. Someone, perhaps the king himself, had told the brawny Highlander that the lad who came to him from Galloway had gifted eyes.

Smiling, he turned on his heel facing the guild hall two hundred yards away. The lettering seemed small, but he rubbed his eyes and looked again, thankful the good fathers of St. Cuthbert's had hammered Latin into his skull.

"What do you see, young sir?" Maclean's voice was neutral, almost disinterested.

"The inscription is composed of three Latin words," Hugh said slowly. *"Industria et labore.* Industry and labor."

"We will take a walk, Hugh Gordon, and I'll see for myself. I understand only Gaelic and broad Scots, but I know Latin when I see it."

When they stood in front of the guild hall, Angus slowly spelled out the letters, "I-n-d-u-s-t-r-i-a!" He turned to Hugh. "There is not a golden eagle in the Isle of Mull can see as far as you, lad. Pardon me for being cautious, but I had to know if you were the one King Robert spoke of. You are that one indeed, but late in arriving."

As they walked back to the inn, Hugh told Black Angus about his head wound at Glen Trool, about the long summer at Glenbirnie, the trap he had escaped at Perth, and the snowstorm he had survived with the help of a shepherd.

Angus shook his head. "These English are clever, like devils from the pit. But we shall beat them, lad. We shall drive them from Scotland and the king will enjoy his own again."

"How is His Highness, Angus?"

Maclean's face clouded. "He has been sore ill, young sir.

When I saw him last, the skin fitted tight over the bones. He has lost weight running from the English in the Highlands, in Erin, in Galloway. Now he is staying quietly at Inverurie, among Scots on whom he can depend."

"But how can I get there? I was to join him as soon as I could and much time has passed."

"Be patient, Hugh Gordon. Some loyal folk in Perth and Forfarshire have information to give me. In a few days we take the road to the north with news for King Robert."

"But how do you know whom to look for and where they will be?"

"Never fear, lad, I have loyal Scots scattered all over this region. They are not nobles, but peasants who watch and hear everything. The shepherd who cared for you last night was one of them. Not a troop of English men-at-arms rides into Perth or Dundee but I have word within twelve hours. These men, risking their lives as spies, bring me reports and information of great value. They are good soldiers even though they never lift a sword or don a coat of mail."

When they had reached the door of the Red Lion under the sign which showed the arms of Scotland, Hugh paused. "Angus, do English soldiers ever come here?"

"Now and then, young sir. But it is a risk one has to take. They drink and carouse in all the hostelries of Dundee."

Hugh went to his room and took a nap. He knew he had two days at least to spend in Dundee. But he did not want to be seen or noticed. A man with a sword was usually of the gentry. English soldiers might stop and question him. Yet without the sword he would have felt practically defenseless on the streets of the town.

He ate dinner that evening with Angus Maclean, then went to bed. The following day, he stood outside the Red

Lion, idly watching the passers-by. Most of the people on the street were Scots, but now and then an English archer in green tunic wandered by. Hugh watched the bowmen with mixed feelings. They were the enemy, but there was a carefree air about them which was attractive to a Scot. Hugh wished the archers of King Robert's army could handle the longbow with the skill of an Englishman.

Standing there for half an hour, Hugh grew bored and turned back toward the door of the inn. A sharp whistle stopped him. He looked around to see Angus Maclean walking swiftly in his direction. His face, usually stern and reserved, was smiling.

"Good news, Angus?"

"Aye, Hugh Gordon." Maclean moved closer, lowering his voice. "We leave early tomorrow morning. For Aberdeenshire. Within forty-eight hours, I promise you, we will be with the king."

"I can't get started too soon, Angus."

There was a low hum of conversation that night, as burghers and travelers mingled in the main room of the inn. The kitchens of the Red Lion had been kept busy preparing food for the hungry. Servingmaids rushed in and out, bearing trays stacked high with food. The smell of beef and mutton filled the air as the guests devoured the contents of huge platters set before them.

Hugh finished his meal and lay back in his chair with an air of contentment. Black Angus drank his mulled wine, his watchful eyes flickering across the room always on guard.

Angus Maclean straightened up in his chair. "I'm for a walk, Hugh Gordon, then to bed. Will you come along?"

"I think I'll stay here, Angus."

"We leave before dawn. I'll see you then." Black Angus drained his tankard and stood up. "I give you good e'en."

Hugh sat quietly for a few minutes watching the crowd, enjoying his hot, spiced drink in the warm room with the cold wind whistling against the frosted windows. The most dangerous part of his mission had been accomplished. He had reached Angus and had been accepted as one of the trusted men of the king.

But his satisfaction was short lived. Before he had finished his ale, a group of English soldiers tramped into the public room and made quickly for a long table next to Hugh's. They were cold and hungry and bawled loudly for the servingmaids.

Some were archers, some men-at-arms. The English had come, twelve in all. Hugh tried to leave quietly, only to find his path blocked by the innkeeper who was escorting a tall, blond English officer in full armor.

"Here is a table, Sir John," the innkeeper said smoothly. "Nobody here but a Scots body already leaving."

"No, no," the Englishman protested. "I pray you, sir, finish your drink. Unless you would not care to sit at table with one of my nation."

The stranger's blue eyes were candid and friendly and Hugh felt a warmth as the Englishman spoke. He had a feeling he would like to know him better. He realized he was playing a dangerous game but he sat down again.

The Englishman ordered his meal and looked across the table at Hugh. "I am Sir John Clifford. Whom do I have the honor of addressing?"

"Hugh Gordon of Glenbirnie, sir."

Sir John's eyes were interested. "I knew you were of gentle birth. Where is Glenbirnie?"

"On the Border, Sir John. I am indeed far from home."

"So am I," the Englishman said saidly. "I have no liking for your cold Scottish winters."

Hugh was tempted to ask Clifford why he did not go

back home, but decided to talk warily, surrounded as he was by English soldiers.

The servingmaid put a haunch of beef before Sir John, who ate as though he had gone without food for a week. Hugh knew he should leave, but wasn't sure just how he could manage it. Besides, he liked Clifford. "Where is your home in England, Sir John?"

Clifford sighed. "In Devon, Gordon of Glenbirnie, where the winter is mild, and the spring as fresh and clean as the apple blossoms which fill our country lanes. Devon is a grand land."

Hugh could not restrain himself. "You have a grand country, Sir John? Why do the English want Scotland, which is a poor country?"

Clifford shot him a quick look. "Why," he said frankly, "I am a soldier. My gracious king, Edward the Second, regards himself as ruler of England, Scotland, and Ireland. And when His Highness orders me to a certain place, I go. Is there anything strange in that?"

"No," Hugh said slowly. "I suppose a soldier must do as he is told. But we Scots, some of us at least, would rather be ruled by our own king."

Sir John finished his beef. "Frankly, Gordon, your argument has merit. If I were a Scot, I might feel as you do. But I am an Englishman."

Hugh drained his tankard. Clifford spoke quickly. "Another drink, my friend. I swear I like thee. If you were not a Scot, we would be the best of companions, Hugh Gordon!"

Hugh accepted another tankard as Clifford ate his way through the heavy meal. Finally he finished, wiping his greasy fingers on a white napkin brought by the servingmaid.

"There," Clifford said jovially. "I have eaten like a man.

My stomach is satisfied." He took a long drink of mulled wine and looked around the room before he turned to Hugh, speaking in a low tone of voice. "Hugh Gordon, I know some Scots hate us, because we have killed and looted. There are men like that, brutal men, in all armies and among all nations. I am a soldier, but I have never been an executioner. Do you believe that?"

"Yes," Hugh said, "I believe you, and I honor you for it. In other times, we could be friends, but, Sir John, I am afraid Scotland has too much to forget."

As he spoke, he heard the clink of spurs on the rough board floor and looked up to see an English officer approaching. There was something faintly familiar about the man's appearance. He was as tall as Sir John and much bulkier, his bloodshot eyes set in a square, swarthy face.

The man paused beside Sir John's chair, his hand falling on Clifford's shoulder. "Good e'en, Sir John."

The tall Englishman looked up. "Oh, yes, Norman. Be seated. This is Hugh Gordon of Glenbirnie. From the Border country, I believe. Norman Bryant."

Hugh stood up, choosing his words carefully. "I'll give up my seat, Sir John, and leave you two alone. I am fagged for lack of sleep."

He felt Bryant's bloodshot eyes fixed firmly on his face, as he bowed and turned to go. A short but powerful arm barred his way. "I have run the fox to earth at last, Clifford."

Bryant's loud voice carried across the room which was suddenly silent. Hugh saw several English soldiers rise from the next table. Out of the corner of his eye he spotted Angus Maclean sitting halfway down the room, watching him intently.

"In the name of the Foul Fiend," Clifford said. "What's the meaning of this, Norman?"

"Why, Sir John, this is the Scot I told you about who escaped me at Perth."

Sir John sprang to his feet. "Did you run from Captain Bryant at Perth the other night?"

Hugh knew he must deny the charges if he were to reach King Robert. "I was in Perth, Sir John, but only on my way to Dundee. I am expected at my grandfather's castle in Aberdeen. He lies gravely ill."

Sir John looked almost believing, but Bryant would have none of it. "He speaks not the truth. This is the man, I tell you. Dick Johnson!"

A tall English archer in Lincoln green stepped forward.

"Is this not the fellow we saw at the Black Boar Inn, the man who leaped his horse into the Tay?"

"Yes, sir. My arrow missed him by inches."

Sir John shook his head. "Hugh Gordon, you may be what you seem, an innocent traveler. But I would be remiss in my duty if I did not send you back to Perth for questioning. It may be you serve the Earl of Carrick some Scots call king."

"They'll get the truth out of this young cockerel at Perth," Bryant said smugly. "Johnson, you and Colson guard the prisoner tonight. We leave at dawn." One of the archers took Hugh's sword, the other searched him for hidden weapons. Then they led him away.

As he went, Hugh saw Angus Maclean and realized the man was trying to send him a message. First Angus elevated a huge fist in the air, then swiftly moved his hand to his mouth, placing his first finger over his lips. He thinks I may talk, Hugh thought dully, but the English will learn nothing from me.

On the stairway he looked back into the big room. Sir John Clifford was standing beside his table with a troubled face. Hugh had the feeling that the likable young Englishman regretted that a war can turn friends into enemies.

Angus of the Ax

Through the long night, Hugh rolled and tossed, leg irons chafing his ankles, anger and disgust rubbing his mind. To think he had been caught here in Dundee after escaping from the English in half a dozen towns. Picked up by accident because an English officer and a bowman had identified him as the fugitive from Perth.

He listened to the archer pacing the watch outside his door. He heard the footsteps of the guard stationed beneath his window. He knew there was no way to escape. Not even Angus Maclean could help him now.

Finally, from sheer exhaustion, Hugh slept, only to be

awakened at dawn by a guard removing his leg irons. "We eat soon, Scot, be ready."

Hugh rolled off the bed, stretching his cramped body. Sleeping in a concealed coat of mail beneath his tunic left him stiff and sore, but better some discomfort than letting the British discover his light armor.

As he was marched to the public room he measured his chances and found them small indeed. If he were lucky he would join that growing army of hostages the English held south of the Border. Or he could swing from the gallows as a spy. His mind reached out quickly to his only hope left—escape. If he were lucky! But how often his father had told him—a man makes his own luck.

Hugh smiled wryly as he sat down at the table where he had so recently eaten wheaten cakes, cheese and mulled wine. Now he ate bread and water as a prisoner.

Bryant, the English officer, watched him with evident satisfaction. "So, my young Scots cockerel, you are not crowing so loudly this fine morning!"

"I am your prisoner, sir," Hugh said, stolidly gnawing his dry bread.

"And like to remain so," was the sharp reply. "If you expect your Earl of Carrick to rescue you, forget it. The man you call king will soon be our prisoner, too. Only when we have caged all the outlaws in Scotland will we be content to go home."

Hugh let the man gloat without the hot reply he might once have made. He would not waste his energies in anger. Well he knew words would not set him free, but the right move at the right time and place.

As though reading Hugh's mind, the Englishman gave a stern warning. "We ride soon to Perth, Scot, and none of your tricks. You will be surrounded. And remember, our bowmen are at their best when shooting at a Scots target!"

Some of the high hope went out of Hugh. He knew now that the tall Englishman hated him and would gladly see him swing on the gallows or be cut to bits by bowmen.

"Sir John Clifford bade me to treat you kindly," Bryant sneered. "He said you were young and, mayhap, innocent of evil intent! Sir John is a good soldier but he is too soft with his enemies. I, my good fellow, do not have that fault."

Hugh could well believe Bryant had few human qualities. As he glanced around the room he was glad Sir John Clifford was not there. He had come to like the tall, open-faced knight.

His liking for Sir John came almost as a surprise, for since childhood Hugh had been taught to hate and fear all Englishmen. Now he knew there were simple, decent English just as there were simple, decent Scots. Suddenly he wanted to be gone so that Sir Clifford would not see him as a prisoner.

He looked across at his ale-drinking guard. "I'm ready when you are."

The bowman wiped his mouth on his coat sleeve. "Riding is cruel sport for me, but in this wild country of yours even archers have to climb into a saddle. Come on."

Hugh refused to give up hope. Somewhere on the road to Perth he must look for his own luck. After all, he knew the country and the customs. The English were in strange territory.

But in spite of his determination to hold fast, Hugh found a lump in his throat as he mounted Sheila in the stable back of the inn. The little mare had so sturdily carried him over the roughest of roads, through storm and sun. If he were to spend the next few years of his life in

an English dungeon, Sheila would join some English
horse herd, never to see the green hills of Galloway again.
Nor would he himself see Glenbirnie Castle.

"On with you, lad," called his guard.

Hugh patted Sheila's neck, picked up the reins and rode
down the narrow main street of Dundee as the column
moved in twos, ten bowmen and men-at-arms headed by
Bryant who turned in his saddle to watch his prisoner.
The men laughed and joked as their quivers bounced on
their backs. To Hugh's practiced eye they were not accustomed to riding like knights. Few of them were even
average horsemen.

Through the dreary day they rode, with the fog rolling
in off the Firth of Tay. Settling miserably into his saddle,
Hugh tried to fight off despair and keep his mind alert,
his eyes sharp for the one chance he wanted.

As the mare plodded down the muddy road, Hugh
began to realize it was strange Angus Maclean had not
even tried to see him. Perhaps the Scot planned a surprise
attack on the road to Perth. But as he watched the English
officer looking sharply up and down the highway, the
hope seemed to grow thinner. Bryant was not the kind
to be caught napping or drawn into ambush.

Riding with his head down against the rain, his legs
warm against Sheila's coat, Hugh was caught unaware by
the order to halt. Filling the road ahead was a large flock
of sheep, a shepherd leading them, a dog bringing up the
rear.

"Get those animals off the road," bellowed Bryant.
"Move, before my men spear them!"

The shepherd turned from the head of the woolly
column and waved his arm. Hugh, tense and alert now,
suddenly felt that wave of the arm was for him. He knew,
even if the English didn't, that a shepherd would not be

moving down this particular road at this time of year. Winter pastures were in the other direction, far off the main highway.

Excitement held him, but carefully he slumped in his saddle pretending complete indifference. Here was his luck, he knew, but how to take advantage of it he could not yet fathom.

The sheep were slogging their way forward, ahead of the English column, with the collie walking sedately behind them. Neither the shepherd nor the dog seemed in any great hurry in spite of Bryant's roars of rage.

Impatiently the English riders slowed their horses to a walk behind the damp white flock as the road ran beside a huge outcropping of granite. Behind it were bushes climbing the hillside and a small glen which ran down to the road.

Still the shepherd ahead moved at a deliberate slow pace until the flock was well past the glen. He seemed utterly deaf to the towering rage of Bryant, who wheeled his horse and rode to the rear of his column. "Jack, Bert, get up front and kill those sheep! And bring me that woolly-witted shepherd. I'll make him remember me for a long time!"

Hugh kept his eyes on the shepherd. Deliberately the man moved his arm again, as if beckoning. This was it. Hugh knew his chance had come. He was being told to ride through the flock. Carefully he looked back and saw the men ordered to slaughter the sheep were riding from the rear of the column.

Then it happened like a bolt from the rain-swept heavens. Into the road leaped a towering figure in shirt of mail, brown-checked kilt and face-concealing hauberk. With two monstrous hands he swung the Lochaber ax of the

Highlands. His clan slogan echoed through the hills. *"Bas no Beatha!"*

His voice like the sound of trumpets brought peasants with spears, scythes, rocks and clubs swarming into the road, taking up the battle cry, *"Bas no Beatha!"* as skulls cracked, metal clanged and horses screamed.

Almost dazed, Hugh watched Angus bring down Bryant and his horse with a crashing blow of his ax. A second man fell under a crunching swing. A third lifted his bow and was cut down. Soldiers and peasants closed in combat as the English were knocked from their saddles. From the bushes high above the granite boulder came a shower of arrows from hidden Scottish archers.

With a guilty start, Hugh realized the fight was for him, a diversion! And there he sat, unarmed like a frozen rabbit. The English at the head of the column had now pulled their horses around and were riding back to the fight. Even his guards, addlewitted by sudden attack, were no longer watching their prisoner.

He knew now what Angus meant him to do. Lying low on Sheila's neck, he dashed ahead into the sheep, dodging arrows, urging the mare on as the woolly animals milled around him in terror.

Covered by the din of battle, Hugh rode halfway through the flock before an English bowman sent a shaft after him. Breathing a prayer, he tugged Sheila to one side as the arrow grazed his shoulder.

The clash of arms grew noisier but Hugh knew he dared not stop. Crouched low over the mare's back, he sent Sheila leaping forward, clearing the backs of rams and ewes too frightened to get out of the way.

He was a moving target now, zigzagging through the sheep as more arrows whizzed past him from the rear. With a final burst of speed Sheila cleared the last ram and pulled out of range just as the shepherd jumped from the side of the road.

"Take me up behind and quickly!"

Hugh pulled in the mare who danced with fear as the old man climbed nimbly behind the saddle. "Hurry, lad, a few yards down the road a path leads to the Ochil hills. Turn off there and the English will ride on to Perth!"

Hugh gave Sheila her head and felt the wet wind sting his face. "Anyone following us?"

"No, lad, the English have lost their officer and don't know which way to turn."

"The man with the Lochaber ax and brown kilt. Angus Maclean?"

"Aye, Black Angus!"

"You know him?"

"I work for him, lad. Here, to the left now."

Hugh swung the mare off the Perth highway and slumped in the saddle as the welcome bushes closed around him. He was still not certain he had escaped the brutal Bryant, but he knew he owed his life to Angus Maclean and the man who rode behind him.

He let Sheila blow after the hard run. "I wish I could have stayed to help Angus, even if I had to use my bare hands!"

The shepherd shook his head. "No, lad, you did exactly what Black Angus wanted you to do. He stationed me here with my sheep to block the road. I signaled you to ride forward if you could. Our Scots were giving the English a hard time and you escaped safe and sound."

"I only hope Angus is safe and sound."

The shepherd put a gentle hand on Hugh's shoulder. "Black Angus has a head too hard to break. Let's get on now. Angus told us to meet him at a cave about ten miles from here."

As they rode, Hugh kept turning around to look for possible pursuers. The shepherd smiled. "Do not fret yourself, lad. You see the sheep dog behind us? If any English horseman appeared he would bark a warning."

Hugh breathed easier and began to look ahead as they wound through the Ochil hills, the sheep track turning and twisting. But Sheila was surefooted in spite of her double burden. It was as though the little mare too realized they had outsmarted the English. Behind them came no jingle of spurs or clang of armor. There was only the quiet of the misty gray hills and the lonely rock-bound land.

After several hours, the shepherd again tapped Hugh's shoulder. "Turn to the right, lad."

Hugh pulled on Sheila's rein and looked up the narrow ravine ahead. Great granite boulders seemed poised on the edge of the ravine as if about to crash down on the helpless traveler.

The shepherd chuckled. "The English will have a hard time finding us here. A man not knowing those rocks are secure would think long before riding up this path. The cave is only a mile now."

The trail became so steep that the little mare began to breathe heavily. Hugh stopped and dismounted. "Get into the saddle and I will walk."

The shepherd slipped his brogues into the stirrups. " 'Tis a rare comfort for an old man. Thank ye for your thoughtfulness. When the king comes into his own again I hope he makes you a knight."

"There's nothing I would like better, but the man who wears the golden spurs of a knight in Scotland must earn them. So far, I have done nothing except get myself captured and put Angus in danger."

"You are young, lad, a stout man and a brave one. Some

day, mark you well, you will wear at the court of King Robert the golden spurs."

Hugh thanked the man kindly, but he knew his chances for such an honor were remote. As a messenger and spy he could not perform feats of arms for his king. Until he could, he knew he would never be a knight in the army of the Bruce.

"Here we are, lad," the shepherd said.

Hugh looked around, seeing only a desolate stretch of rocky hills. There was no sign of a cave, but to the right of the ravine a clump of bushes seemed patched to the cliff.

The shepherd dismounted, pushed the bushes aside and guided Hugh through the concealed entrance and down steps carved from stone to a small spring whose water bubbled invitingly. On the other side of the spring a narrow entrance loomed in a rocky recess.

" 'Tis narrow, lad. Turn sideways." Hugh followed the shepherd's example and squeezed through the rocks, his shirt scraping the stone. Suddenly he was in complete darkness. The shepherd was gone.

Then a voice called, "Come forward."

Inching his way along, his hand over his head to warn him of low-hanging rocks, Hugh made his way toward the voice. After what seemed an endless time, the passageway widened suddenly into a cave and Hugh could see the shepherd seated by a small fire whose smoke found its way to the sky through a hole in the rocky roof.

"Your voice sounded strange in this place. Angus is not here?"

"Aye, we are ahead of Black Angus."

"If he comes at all."

"Do not be in such a hurry, lad. I know Black Angus. He will stay until the last head is cracked."

Hugh waited an anxious hour, while the shepherd dozed

beside him. Finally, he could stand it no longer. Carefully he felt his way out of the cave and looked into the late afternoon light. Angus had not yet appeared.

The waiting and loneliness stretched his heart thin. He crossed the narrow road where the mare was grazing among the boulders. "You and I got away, Sheila. But Angus may lie bleeding and mortally hurt on the road to Perth. My freedom may have come high for him. Yet here I wait, without so much as a sword or knife!"

Sheila looked at him with sympathy and nuzzled his hand. Then her ears came forward in alarm at the faint and distant sound of clinking arms. Hugh listened too. It could be Angus. Or it could be the English. Quickly he untied Sheila. If the newcomers were English, the least he could do was to ride Sheila up the road and draw the enemy away from the cave and the sleeping shepherd.

Grimly he turned the mare into the sheep track and waited. Far down the road now he could see figures coming into view up the narrow glen. His keen eyes saw that at least one supported himself on a spear as though it were a crutch. Several were limping. At least two wore bandages red with blood. Ahead of the group towered a broad-shouldered giant who half lifted, half carried with him a smaller man.

"Angus, Angus Maclean!" he shouted, and rushed on foot down the trail toward the man who had bought freedom for Hugh Gordon of Glenbirnie.

The Road to Inverurie

There was a smile on Angus Maclean's dark face as he saw Hugh race toward him.

"Let me help you with yon man, Angus! Grateful I am to you for life itself," Hugh shouted as he rushed down the path to offer the wounded man his arm. "I was sore worried, Angus, and a bit ashamed."

"Ashamed! Why, Hugh Gordon?"

"I did not do much to save myself."

"Ye did exactly right. I planned the surprise attack, placing the shepherd to the front, where he could beckon you. I knew with your keen eyes you would understand the signal, and you did."

"Are't wounded, Angus?"

"A few hard knocks, but no blood lost. My friend here and one other bringing up the rear have been hurt badly, though. Fortunately our sheepherder is good at bandaging wounded men."

The Scots in Angus' band, plodding up the path, looked curiously at Hugh. He was the man they had rescued. They had never seen him before. They would never see him again. But they recognized in him a friend of the Bruce. For them that was enough.

Nearing the bushes at the cave's entrance, Angus glanced sharply at Sheila munching grass on the other side of the road. "I see you brought the mare with you, Hugh. I had a horse hidden back in the trees where we attacked the English. But he was not tied well and bolted. So here I am, on foot."

"You can ride Sheila," Hugh offered.

"Mayhap I will, if my big feet get too tired. However, these brogues have carried me over most of Scotland and part of England, so I'll wait awhile before burdening your horse with my huge carcass."

Slowly and carefully Angus and Hugh half-carried the wounded man between them down the rocky steps to the cave's mouth. Angus, familiar with the place, went ahead, leaving Hugh to steady the wounded man through the narrow entrance.

The small cavern was crowded, but the smell of mutton stew cooking slowly in a huge pot over the fire was welcome to the hungry men. The shepherd stirred the savory contents of the pot and beamed with pleasure at the newcomers. "*Cead mille failte*, Black Angus!"

"What is he saying in Gaelic, Angus?" Hugh whispered.

"It means 'a hundred thousand welcomes.'"

Angus looked down at the wounded man he and Hugh had brought to the cave. The Scot was lying on the rocky floor, eyes half-closed. Angus beckoned a redheaded boy in a blue and green kilt. "Watch the stew, lad. We need the shepherd as a doctor here."

Some of the men brought forward the other wounded fighter, and they were placed side by side on a plaid spread out close to the fire, where the old man inspected the crimson bandages as Hugh held a lighted pine knot.

After a swift inspection, the sheepherder bathed the wounds and replaced the bandages.

"How badly are they hurt?" Angus asked.

"One will be up and around in a day or so. The other must be quiet for weeks. A savage cut heals slowly."

"Can you stay here and care for them, old man?"

"My sheep are scattered, Angus, and I work for my Lord Murray. If one of your lads could stay with me for a few days, I could find my flock with my dog's help, and drive it up this track, where they can graze close by. But I fear me the sheep are lost."

"You go and find your sheep, man," Angus said. "I'll have a lad stay here and nurse the wounded while you're gone. I must be off to Inverurie with the lad here. I have information for King Robert."

"Good," Hugh said. "You shall ride Sheila, while I walk."

"We'll take turns. Our shanks may wear out before we reach the king. We'll have to go by way of the sheep tracks back in the hills. Our shortest road would be through Aberdeen, but the town is filled with English— and Scots traitors." There was a note of bitterness in Angus' voice.

"You know, Hugh, John Comyn, the Earl of Buchan, at Aberdeen is a friend of the English. He hates the Bruce, so much so that when his wife, Isabella, placed the crown on the king's head at Scone, Buchan was beside himself with rage. And he urged the English to punish her severely."

"I remember her," Hugh said quickly. "I was a lad at Scone when it happened. She was a beautiful woman, like a queen."

"Aye," Black Angus said. "For four years now she has been a prisoner at Berwick-on-Tweed. The English put that lovely bird in a cage. I mean that, Hugh. Her prison is a long room, partly inside the wall of the castle. One end, ringed with iron bars, projects from the wall. I was in Berwick a year ago, and I saw that great lady standing there on that platform, looking toward Scotland and the North."

"Her husband must be a monster," Hugh said hotly.

"Greedy, that's all. Like so many of the nobles. They do not want to risk their landed estates by fighting for the Bruce. As for me, I have nothing to lose—except my life."

The low hum of conversation from the men around the fire gradually died away and Hugh watched them drop off into heavy sleep, exhausted from the battle. He talked to Black Angus in whispers. "I am truly grateful for my rescue, but sorry that Scots were wounded in my behalf. I saw you knock the English captain, Bryant, from his horse. Is he dead?"

"That I would not know," Angus said dryly. "I was too busy laying about with my ax. I know I emptied three saddles and my spearmen accounted for two more. The surviving English fled back toward Dundee."

"It seems impossible," Hugh said. "There were a dozen Englishmen, well trained in the art of war. You were the only experienced soldier among the Scots, isn't that true, Angus? The rest were countrymen and boys."

"They were not skilled, but they had the will to fight,

lad. These peasants, as the English call them, are accustomed to hard knocks. A surprise attack confuses even
the best of troops, but if that captain you call Bryant had
not been put out of action early in the fight, it might have
been a different story."

"Bryant hates all Scots. He had never seen me before,
but he hated me. He could hardly wait to get me to Perth
for questioning."

"That he will never do, Hugh. What of that other
Englishman you met in Dundee, was he like Bryant?"

"Not at all, Angus, a kindly man and well mannered."

"I have never met a kindly Englishman," Angus grunted.
"But I'm glad you have. Now let's get some sleep. We
start early in the morning."

As he dressed in the half-light of dawn, Hugh was again
irked by the loss of his sword, not only a weapon but a
symbol of the wellborn. Then he remembered that men
without blades had wrought his rescue, honest Scots who
regarded him as a brother in the great fight for freedom.
He was ashamed of himself, and decided he would carry
the dirk or knife of the peasants as a protection—and as a
badge of honor.

Others were rising around him when he heard Angus'
deep voice on the other side of the fire. "Lads, we've been
through a sharp fight, and you have done well. Now's the
time to scatter, though. Get ye gone to your hills and
remember that, one day again, Angus Maclean may have
need of thee."

There was a muffled cheer, and the big Highlander
raised his hand again. "Thank ye, lads. Hugh Gordon,
whom we rescued yesterday, is grateful for your help and
will commend your loyal service to the king himself when
we reach Aberdeenshire. God keep you all!"

Wolfing down their breakfasts, they crawled from the cave, leaving the shepherd and one of the younger boys to care for the wounded.

Hugh crossed the road and took the hobbles off Sheila, grazing on the meager grass. Then he mounted and turned the mare to the left. He looked down at Angus walking briskly beside Sheila in the chill air, and was thankful that his hose and tunic were good wool.

He stared at Angus' brawny bare knees below the kilt and marveled at the man's indifference to cold. Hugh wondered where the big Scot had abandoned his Lochaber ax, for he carried now a great bow with a quiver of arrows at his back. "Angus, I lost my sword at Dundee, when I was captured. I have not even a knife to defend myself."

The Highlander bent over and pulled a dirk from his woolen stocking. "Here is mine, Hugh. I will make out very well with the bow here."

"What if we meet up with the English?"

"Not in these hills. We are heading for Inverurie on sheep tracks the English do not know exist."

"But the Scots at Aberdeen, like Buchan, surely know the paths and passes hereabouts."

"They may stumble onto us when we get farther north. If they do, we must fight or run. 'Tis better to run, since I bear the king tidings. Furthermore, I want to deliver you safely to the Bruce."

They kept to the north now, the path winding between granite boulders and loose rock. In the background, Hugh could see an occasional fir tree standing like a lone sentinel. The sky was a dull gray with only a few birds floating lazily aloft.

After another hour, Hugh offered to let Angus ride

Sheila, but the Highlander refused. "I keep warm walking, Hugh. Besides, I'm not tired. We have a few shaggy ponies in the Isle of Mull where I was born, but most Macleans use their two feet to get from one place to another."

"Angus, what was that slogan you cried when you felled Bryant on the road to Perth? I know only a little Gaelic."

"The clan cry of the Macleans. '*Bas no Beatha.*' It means 'Death or Life.' "

"Death or Life," Hugh said slowly. "That is what war means, is it not, Angus?"

"Aye, lad. That is war. My father died in battle. It may be so with me."

Hugh's face had sobered and Angus changed the subject. "We are heading for Forfar, lad, but we'll circle around the place, then go to Brechin on the South Esk River. I want to cross the North Esk as soon as possible and reach Fettercairn."

"Is that the safe road to the north, Angus?"

"No road is a safe road this close to Aberdeen. From Fettercairn, we will head for the pass of Cairn-a-Mounth, staying away from the coast, lad. Once safely through the pass, we can angle northwest to the Dee River. Beyond the Dee lies Corrichie and beyond Corrichie is the Don River, and there, at Inverurie, we will find King Robert."

They ate bread and cheese at noon, then continued their journey through the wild and desolate country stretching to Cairn-a-Mounth. It was a trip Hugh would not soon forget. At night they lay on a hillside well back from the road they had been following, waking cold and hungry in the morning. By day they traveled cautiously, now and then finding a shepherd's hut where they could buy food.

Occasionally they passed rude cottages of rough stone, where women came to the door and eyed them curiously.

Angus spoke to them in Gaelic, and they smiled. One called them inside and gave them a meal of cold milk and wheaten cakes, with oats for Sheila in the byre out back. Hugh thought he had never eaten food so good.

Hugh and Angus, alternately riding and walking, finally reached Corrichie just before nightfall. The villagers looked suspiciously at them as they passed through the only street, but asked no questions. On the edge of town, Angus stopped at a peasant's cottage and bought some oatmeal. Under a larch tree on a high hill, Angus and Hugh made camp under the cold stars.

Angus baked cakes on his iron skillet. They drank cold water from a nearby spring, then lay down on the earth and slept heavily beside the dying fire.

At daybreak they tightened their belts and rode on. "We'll reach the Don River late tonight and cross over to Inverurie," Angus said. " 'Tis a good thing you are young and stout, lad. Even I am tired."

Just after the noon hour, they reached the Don. Angus looked up and down the river. "I have a feeling that all is not right here," he said slowly. "That road on the north side of the river might well be used by the English at Aberdeen."

"Why, Angus?"

"Because Inverurie lies back in the hills, above it. To strike at the Bruce, Buchan and the English might well choose this road for a surprise attack."

Angus sat down on the ground and stretched out. "We will stay here until after nightfall. Tie Sheila to a bush, so she will be well concealed from eyes across the river."

The Highlander bent over and put his ear to the earth, listening intently. "I was right, Hugh. A large body of men is moving up that road across the Don."

"You think they're English?"

"They must be, coming from the direction of Aberdeen."

"That means they intend to attack the king," Hugh said. "Can we warn him, Angus?"

"Not now. If we tried to swim the Don, we'd reach the opposite bank just when the English were moving up. No, our job is not to warn the king. He has scouts who have no doubt told him of Buchan's approach."

They lay on the cold ground, peering across the river. Soon Hugh's sharp eyes caught sight of English riders moving up, an advance guard of men-at-arms. Behind them rode knights in full armor, lances at rest. Bringing up the rear were English archers in Lincoln green, with a scattering of Scots.

Hugh could see the faces of the knights clearly. One of them, a tall man with a thin face and hawk's nose, especially attracted his attention. The rider had a cruel thin-lipped mouth and cold blue eyes. From time to time, he turned in his saddle to inspect the army marching along behind him.

"Angus, I can see one of their leaders very plainly." Hugh described the man with the cold eyes.

"That would be John Comyn, the Earl of Buchan himself. Would that my arrows could span the Don. I would almost give my life for one fair shot at the traitor."

Hugh watched the army march briskly to the west along the Don, disappearing around the bend of the river. "I count around eight hundred of them, Angus."

"Aye. That force is not strong enough to defeat the king. Buchan may well live to regret this foray against the Red Lion of Scotland."

"I hope so. How do we reach our Scots camp?"

"We'll cross the river five miles to the west and circle

around, entering Inverurie from the north. Buchan will attack from the south, up a glen which runs down to the road about a mile from here." He sighed. "We will miss the battle, but it is more important to reach the king with a whole skin."

The dark gray afternoon blended into twilight as they crossed to the north bank of the Don. Even after nightfall Angus kept moving doggedly on, with Hugh behind him on Sheila. The Highlander seemed to know every obscure path and sheep track in Aberdeenshire.

About midnight, Angus halted. "We'll sleep for a few hours, lad, and be on our way."

It was noon before they looked down on Inverurie from a neighboring hill. At one end of the town campfires blazed in a big field. Men in kilts and armor wandered through the streets.

Hugh shouted joyfully, "King Robert holds Inverurie! That means Jock Lockhart is down there. The Bruce has beaten Buchan!"

"You must be right. Let's join the army and borrow some oaten meal. I'm fair famished."

A picket challenged them on the rim of the campfires, but identified Angus as they approached.

"Glad I am to see you, Maclean," the sentry said.

"This is Hugh Gordon with me. We were hidden on the south bank of the Don when Buchan's army marched by on the other side of the river. What happened?"

"We hit the English hard at Old Meldrum, four miles to the south. A great victory for King Robert. It convinced many of these nobles in the north that the Bruce will win. The gentry have been coming into town by the dozen, to swear allegiance."

"Where is the king, Lockhart?" asked Angus.

"You just passed the house he is using for headquarters. His Highness is still far from well, but he mounted his charger last night, like the noble knight he is, and rode hard into the ranks of the English. Today he is resting."

"I have news for him," Angus said. "It cannot wait."

A Spy for Scotland

Hugh and Angus, ushered into the presence of the king, found the Bruce reclining on a deerskin placed on a low couch against the farmhouse wall. Each went down on one knee, as was the custom, but the king waved them to their feet.

"Right glad I am to see both of you," Robert said, his blue eyes alight. He looked at Hugh. "Was it difficult to find Angus Maclean, huge hulk that he is?" The king's tone was warm and friendly.

"I had a hazardous journey to Dundee, Your Highness, but my perils were of my own making."

"Some day, when I have time, you must tell me about them. The important thing is that you are here, Hugh Gordon."

"I would not be here without the help of Angus Mac-lean," Hugh said quickly. "A few days ago, I was a pris-oner of the English, on my way to an English dungeon. Angus and some hardy Scots rescued me, for which I will be forever grateful."

"Angus has rescued many a man to fight for Scotland," the king said. "He has ears that work for me, and an ax as well."

"My ax and my ears are always at the service of my king," Angus said. "The lad, here, is a good man, Your Highness, though a bit young. His eyesight is as good as you said it was."

The king looked at the big Highlander. "I would have your reports now, sir. Gordon can wander around the town and come back in an hour."

As Hugh left the farmhouse, he found himself for the first time in many days with no pressing business and no English breathing down his neck. Slowly he strolled around the camp watching soldiers practicing their skills, building cook fires, and sharpening their axes. He felt alone, for all were strangers with whom he had nothing in common except loyalty to a beleaguered king.

Thinking his own thoughts, walking aimlessly, he al-most ran into a man with his arm in a sling, and looked into the face of Jock Lockhart.

"Jock! I thought never to see you again! And you are wounded?"

"A trifle, lad, nothing so serious as that knock on the head you got at Glen Trool. That Highlander with you, Black Angus, is something of a legend in our army. He is here, there and everywhere. Seems a shame to waste his talents as a spy, though. He fights like a man possessed!"

"Aye, he handles a Lochaber ax like a willow wand."

"That I know, lad. Tales reached us of his fight when

he rescued you on the road to Perth. I wish I could have seen it, or much better, felled a few Englishmen myself."

Hugh and Jock walked down the street to the only tavern in Inverurie and there drank mulled wine and discussed the war.

"I suppose you noticed that the king does not look too well."

"Yes," said Jock. "He fought hard yesterday, but the years have taken a heavy toll. He's been hounded all over Scotland. His queen is a prisoner of the English, as is his daughter. He's eaten only where he could find food, usually sharing it with a common soldier. Where but in Scotland could you find such a king?"

They sat for a few minutes, lost in admiration for a king without a throne. Around them crowded bowmen, axmen and a sprinkling of young men-at-arms. Jock nodded in their direction. "Those men are pages and esquires, men who hope some day to become knights."

"Even as I do, Jock."

"I can understand that ambition, Hugh, but it's a hard road. I was once a page myself, then an esquire. But I have been in battle rather than at court. I doubt if I will ever wear the golden spurs of a knight."

"Of course you will, Jock. And I will be the first to wish you well when you are dubbed knight by the king."

"I hope you are right, Hugh Gordon, but I have watched the rise of men to knighthood. Usually, they are those who have distinguished themselves at court, or soldiers who have done great feats in battle. I'm afraid I have done neither, and am not likely to with my arm in a sling."

Hugh put down his empty mug. "You are too modest, Jock. You just need an opportunity to show what you can do. I'd best be going. I'm to meet Angus at the king's headquarters before sundown."

As Hugh waited at the farmhouse for Angus, Sir James
Douglas emerged and gave welcome. "I hear you've served
our king well, Hugh Gordon. You have used not only your
gifted eyes but your sharp wits. Go in, now, the Bruce
would see you."

"Thank you, Sir James."

When he entered the now-familiar room he saw Angus
standing beside the window and the Bruce sitting on the
low couch, his face flushed and eager. "Come in, Hugh.
Angus and I have been speaking of you."

The king raised himself on one elbow. "I have already
talked this matter over with Angus. He tells me that you
and he have discussed the sad fate of my loyal friend
Isabella, Countess of Buchan."

"Yes, sire. I saw her put the royal crown on your head."

"It seems a long time ago." The king sighed. "How my
friends have suffered for their devotion to me! The countess is wife, as you know, to the ruffianly Earl of Buchan
whose forces I defeated yesterday. He is such a villain
that he would have allowed the English to execute the
countess for the act of crowning me at Scone."

"Sire, in Galloway we would hold that such a man had
basely betrayed the woman he had sworn to love and
cherish."

"That is true, Hugh Gordon. I have a plan, and I want
you to help Angus carry it out. We talked once before
about serving Scotland, and we agreed that a man could
greatly aid his country without fighting for it. I will add
your name to the roster of my pages, then send you on an
errand with Maclean here. It will be a daring venture, and
both of you will take your lives in your hands. What say
you, man of Galloway?"

"I say Yes, sire."

"Good, Hugh Gordon. You will not be forgotten by the

Bruce when we drive the English from our country." The king leaned closer. "I want you and Angus to go to Berwick and see if you cannot find a way to get a message to the countess to let her know the Bruce has not forgotten her."

Hugh's amazement was mirrored in his eyes. "But the countess is imprisoned in the castle at Berwick-on-Tweed."

"That is right. Angus thinks that the two of you can devise a scheme to reach Countess Isabella."

"By your leave, sire," Angus said. "How well can you climb, Hugh Gordon?"

"Climb!" Hugh said. "Why, well enough, I guess. I have done my share of climbing in the hills of Galloway."

"I thought it possible, lad. You may have to ascend the wall of Berwick Castle to reach the countess. What think you of that kind of climbing?"

"I will try anything, Angus!"

"A lad of proper spirit, sire," Angus said. "I will explain my plan to young Gordon as we go south."

"God's blessing on you both." King Robert tore a link from the golden chain around his neck. "Give this to the countess, Gordon of Glenbirnie, if you get in touch with her. That will identify you as my agent. Angus, report back to me at Ayr. Our army marches south in a few days, to harry the English in Galloway. Be careful, both of you."

As they left, Hugh turned to Angus. "When do we leave?"

"Early tomorrow. I must find you a sword, somewhere."

"Jock Lockhart can get one."

"Good. See Jock and make sure your horse has plenty of food. We must ride far and fast."

Before the sun was up, Hugh was ready and eager for the open road. When Angus came back from the other

side of town, riding a big iron gray, Hugh showed him
the blade he had borrowed the night before. Carefully
Angus inspected the sword. "It will do, lad. Until we
reach Kelso."

"What mean you, Angus, until we reach Kelso?"

"We leave our horses there and go to Berwick on foot,
driving a small herd of cattle. You'll get used to the
beasties, never fear." Angus looked at Hugh's crestfallen
face. "Come, come, lad, use your wits. We do not ride
boldly in among the English, sword in hand. We are
spies, and we will be in Berwick for one purpose only,
to see if we can get word to the countess of King Robert's
interest in her welfare."

"Of course, Angus. I was stupid."

Jock Lockhart came up to bid them farewell.

"Good-by, Jock," Hugh said. "If the army ever reaches
Galloway, visit Glenbirnie, if you can. My father will welcome you. And tell him I am serving the king."

"Aye, lad. Good-by."

Hugh long remembered that ride to the Border country. Angus, anxious to reach his destination, made few
stops. Only when they reached Kelso did Angus agree
to rest. There they camped in a bend of the river and
watched bands of sheep browsing on the first shoots of
spring grass, with an occasional Border collie gravely
watching his charges. When Hugh saw a dog like that, a
lump came to his throat as he thought of Jamie frisking
beside Loch Urr, of his father dozing in his big oak chair
before the fire, of Thomas Dickson and his wife. Home
to him was still a place where serenity and peace reigned.

As they rode into town, Hugh looked cautiously at the
shops fronting on the big market square, but Angus had
eyes only for a stone farmhouse by the bridge spanning
the Tweed. Here they were admitted by a tall sandy-

haired Scot who helped Hugh get rid of his mail tunic and pull a long green smock over his hose.

"Ye look like a drover now, young sir," the farmer said, "as does the kilted one here." The man grinned at Angus who had donned a red and green kilt.

"Is that your clan tartan?" Hugh asked. Angus laughed. "No, it's the MacDougall. Both are red and green. If some officer in Berwick asks me, I'll tell him I'm a Mac-Dougall. That clan is friendly to the English. If a Scot asks me, I'll say I'm a Maclean, friendly to the king."

Satisfied with their appearance, Hugh and Angus ate the hearty meal offered by their host and bedded down on the floor of the main room.

Angus shook Hugh awake before the cock crowed. "Work to be done, lad. You are no longer a king's man, but a drover. You will walk from Kelso to Berwick. We're leaving the horses here. They will have good care. Now, look alive, lad."

In the pleasant spring sunshine, Hugh found himself ambling along the Tweed with Angus behind a small herd of shaggy red cattle, heading for Berwick. The cattle moved slowly, trying to munch grass along the road, prevented by Angus who swung his staff and bawled at them in Gaelic.

It was thus that Hugh Gordon of Glenbirnie came to the great city of Berwick-on-Tweed, not riding Sheila, a sword at his thigh and a mailed shirt on his back, but dressed like a lowly Scots farmer.

He gaped like a country boy at the great commercial town he had heard of but never seen. It fronted for four miles on the Tweed. To the east was the North Sea. Surrounding Berwick was a stout wall with high towers. Beside the Tweed itself rose the many-storied castle, with its famous Water Tower and two flanking bastions.

The castle looked dark and evil even in the faint sunlight which tried to break through the gray afternoon. Hugh lifted his eyes toward the great keep where Isabella MacDuff, now Countess of Buchan, was imprisoned. It was his job to reach her, if possible, by bribing an attendant at the castle, or by scaling the wall of the castle itself if necessary.

English guards looked at them without curiosity as Angus herded the steers rapidly through the steep, cobbled streets until he reached wooden cattle pens close to the river.

He left Hugh for a short time to hold the herd together, and returned with a broad smile on his face. "I've sold the beasties, lad. I'll let down the bars and we'll put them in the nearest pen. Then we'll find a tavern and look around. At night, mind you, a Highlander can see in the dark like a cat."

"Have you found out anything, Angus?"

"Only that the Countess of Buchan is still here. Townsfolk can see her as she walks back and forth on an iron porch jutting out from the castle wall. The porch has bars and a roof. A cage for a lovely lady."

As they walked toward the low-roofed tavern at one end of a muddy street, Angus frowned. "We will have to do it the hard way," he said. "I have inquired about the folks in the castle. They are all English, not a single Scot among them. Which means that we cannot find a man to bear the countess our message, even if we could trust him, which I doubt."

"Then it's up the castle wall for me," Hugh said.

"All in good time. Let's put our gear in the inn. Then we'll hire a boat and float down the river, past the keep."

An hour later, they had cast off from the bank, and Angus, rowing with powerful strokes, had sent the skiff dancing down the Tweed. He kept to the middle of the river, then shipped oars and picked up a fishing pole. "We'll drift toward the castle, lad, and pretend we're catching trout. There may be sentries on the walls who will watch us closely."

Slowly the skiff drifted in toward the Berwick bank, Angus apparently busy with the pole. "What see you with those hawk's eyes, lad?"

Hugh had been watching the wall intently. "It can be scaled, Angus—at night, of course. There are small stones projecting beyond the main rampart. You can barely see them because they are covered with ivy. Yes, the wall can be climbed. Look, Angus, there is the enclosure in which the English keep the countess."

"I dare not look, lad. And do not gawk. A man who stares overlong at that cage may find himself in a dungeon."

"The ivy is thick below that iron porch, Angus. Even at night, I think I could reach the place. With the aid of Saint Andrew!"

"We will come back tonight," Angus said, laying his fishing pole on the bottom of the boat and taking up the oars. "And we have much to do before we return."

Back on land, Angus took Hugh straight to a forge operated by a Scots blacksmith, an elderly man with gnarled hands who seemed to know Angus well. The smith went into the back room and came out with an iron hook twelve inches long. At the base of the hook there was an eye in which a knot could be tied.

As Hugh watched with interest, Angus produced a rough rope and ran one end of it through the eye of the hook. Next he attached a stout cord to the other end of the rope. Hugh could not contain his curiosity. "What are you doing, Angus? Why is this hook necessary?"

"You will see," Angus said patiently. "If you climb the
wall and find yourself too far from the cage I will cry
out like a black diver, a bird found only in the North of
Scotland. The countess, being northern bred, will hear
the cry and know it comes from a friend, for certainly
there are no black divers in this part of the country. When
she comes out on the porch of her cage you will be close
enough to talk with her. Ask her to go inside and then I
will shoot an arrow through the bars onto the floor. Tell
her to run out quickly and seize the arrow. The light cord
will be attached to it. Then she can pull up the strong rope
and finally the hook."

Hugh nodded toward the old man at the back of the
room.

"He is one of us," Angus said. "Now, to continue. The
countess is to circle one of the bars with this iron hook,
take off the cord which will fall into the Tweed, and
throw you the rope's end. Using that rope you can pull
yourself up close to the cage and talk. Otherwise, you
might find yourself shouting loud enough to bring down
on us every Englishman in Berwick Castle. You understand the plan, lad?"

Hugh nodded, lost, grateful for the canny Highlander
who had planned every detail.

"Now to get this gear to the boat." Angus took off his
tunic and wound the rope and cord around his body,
sticking the hook in his belt. "So, I look like a man who
has long eaten too well!" He raised his voice. "Robbie,
the bow!"

The smith brought a bow and quiver of arrows.

"You can find anything in Berwick if you know where
to look!" Angus winked at Hugh. "Thank you kindly,
Robbie!"

He stuck the bow and quiver into a bundle of faggots.

"Now we are ready, lad. If we had a light, we'd have a fire. Any English sentry stopping us would see only two honest farmers carrying fuel to warm themselves."

They started down the street toward the wharf where they had left the boat. "Hungry, Hugh?"

"I could eat a bit."

"There's bread and cheese in a package lying in the skiff. We'll eat there. It's getting dark and we must be about our business. We've no time to loll at ease in a tavern."

When they reached the skiff, Angus eased the bundle of faggots to the floor of the boat, stepping down beside it. Hugh followed, untying the mooring rope.

"We're on our way lad," Angus said. "In an hour we will know whether we can reach the countess with the king's message."

The Cage of the Countess

"Take the oars, lad," Angus said as the skiff drifted closer to the shadow cast by the massive battlements of Berwick Castle. "I have work to do."

Hugh, sculling the boat now and then, watched attentively as Angus took an arrow from his quiver and encircled the point with a wad of wool. "If it strikes an iron bar, it will fall noiselessly back into the Tweed. If it passes between the bars, into the cage, so much the better."

"You think of everything!"

"One must, in this business." Angus seized the oars and again allowed the boat to move closer to the castle. "I'll put you ashore here, then pull away after you start your

118

climb. There is moonlight on the water, thanks to the
blessed Saint Columba, moonlight enough for me to see
the flight of an arrow."

Hugh did not take his eyes from the parapet as the
boat neared the bank. He knew that English sentries
were on guard high above the Countess Isabella's prison,
but they would not be looking down, for her cage was
located on the water side, overlooking the river. Any
English man-at-arms would be expecting an attack in
force only from the land side. Yet Hugh was well aware
that the slightest noise on his part would draw the attention of the guards.

As the skiff touched the bank, Angus leaped ashore with
a stout rope which he attached to a bunch of faggots.
"Here is our anchor, such as it is, lad," he whispered.
"Are't sure there's enough ivy on that wall for a safe
climb?"

"Enough, I think." Hugh's tone was more confident
than he felt. "There are stones projecting from the main
wall, here and there. See?" He guided Angus' hand to a
point slightly higher than his own head.

"Be up with you, then." Angus bent his broad back for
a ladder, and Hugh clawed his way up the ivy-covered
wall to the first jutting stone, his hand feeling ahead for
enough ivy to carry him three feet higher to the next
narrow ledge.

As the soft pad of Angus' footsteps died away, Hugh
knew he was alone in the soft darkness, clinging to the
vast expanse of ivy. If a single cluster of the vines gave
way, he would be thrown headlong into the river. Guards
would shout, arrows would whiz in his direction, the entire
garrison would be suddenly on the alert.

Blindly his strong fingers closed over the third stone
jutting out into the darkness. Facing the wall, he looked

upward and to the left. The cage of the countess he could see, but it seemed very far away. He had climbed about one fourth of the necessary distance.

Hugh clung to the heavy vines and rested, his forehead beaded with sweat, the palms of his hands moist. He prayed to God and Saint Andrew, then started his climb again. He no longer looked down. Sure-footed and silent in the darkness, he swung upward, climbing, then resting, his muscles taut and tired, his bleeding fingers searching blindly above his head for fresh handholds among the leaves.

It took a long time, a long time to move quietly and carefully. Every time he grasped a clump of ivy, he gave a slight tug to see that it was firmly attached. As he found the stones projecting from the wall, he tested each, leaning heavily to make sure they would not crumble suddenly and throw him into the river below.

Now and then he paused to listen, but heard only the sound of his own labored breathing and the clink of metal as the sentries moved about on the flat stone roof behind the parapet. The Englishmen were not even looking at the river. Angus had been right. No sentry suspected a messenger could reach the Countess Isabella.

Hugh steadied his breathing and inched his way upward toward the cage. Only ten feet more to go, then, reaching out for a handhold, he suddenly found nothing. Even the ivy was scanty. There were no more jutting stones, just the flat smooth surface of the wall itself. He had gone as far as he could possibly go.

Crouched there among the vines, he looked up at the cage of the countess in the pale silver moonlight. In that part of her quarters which lay inside the castle wall, Hugh could make out the glow cast by a candle in its sconce on the wall. The rustling noises and movements in the inner room told him that the countess was still awake.

Every second counted now. Hugh gripped the vines and waved one arm vigorously. From the darkness below came a bird call. Angus had seen him and was imitating a night diver. He listened again as the Highlander repeated the call. Suddenly a woman dressed in white appeared on the iron platform jutting out from the castle wall. She rested her hands on the iron bars, poised, staring intently at the dark water below. He felt sure that Angus, standing upright in the skiff, could see her.

Hugh started to speak, then buried his head in the ivy as an English sentry passed by overhead, his sword clinking against the parapet. He wondered if the Countess Isabella had any chamberwomen in the inside room, Englishwomen who might hear his voice. He decided he would have to take that risk.

"Miladi! Miladi Countess!" he called, his voice scarcely more than a husky whisper. The woman on the iron platform started, then turned around deliberately, erect and proud, walking to the near side of the cage.

"Who calls Isabella, Countess of Buchan?" she asked softly.

"Hugh Gordon of Glenbirnie, Your Ladyship. I bear you a message from King Robert."

"From the Bruce!" Hugh thought he could see her eyes flash in the darkness.

"Yes, Your Ladyship. Do you have English servants inside the door?"

"Only a chamberwoman who is fast asleep."

"Good. Below, in a boat, I have a friend who will shoot an arrow onto the floor of the platform where you now stand. Go inside, miladi, and wait. When the arrow strikes the floor, pick it up. There will be a light cord attached.

Pulling that cord up, you will find a heavier rope beneath it, with an iron hook. You understand, Countess?"

"Yes. I will retire at once, Gordon of Glenbirnie." Her white-robed figure left the iron-barred platform. Hugh waited patiently for Angus to shoot. In seconds, the arrow flew between two of the bars and fell soundlessly on the platform. Hugh crouched against the dark wall and waited.

When the countess came out and picked up the arrow, Hugh could not see clearly, but he noticed she was pulling on the cord. There was silence, then a clank of iron on iron. The countess said something under her breath.

"Is aught wrong, Your Ladyship?"

"I am stupid. Pulling the hook in, I struck it against one of the bars. Has that sentry returned?"

"No, miladi."

"What shall I do with the hook?"

"Encircle one of the bars with it, wedging it securely. Then take the end of the rope, not the cord, and throw it toward me, through the bars on this side. I am hanging to the ivy here, some ten feet from the platform. I must swing up to the floor of the cage if I am to give you my message."

"You climbed that wall, Gordon of Glenbirnie! It is a miracle of skill. You must be an agile young man."

"It is only that I am young, Countess, and I have had some experience. Now, the rope, if it please you."

Isabella of Buchan sent the rope whistling through the air alongside the wall to which Hugh clung. Her first cast missed. She tried again—and again. The fourth time, Hugh's fingers gripped it tightly. He swung off from the ivy-covered wall and danced on the air, pulling himself up to the cage hand over hand.

Feeling above his head in the darkness, he touched the

bottom of the platform, then swung himself higher until one of his hands grasped one iron bar, then another. The bars were six inches apart. Hugh slowly drew himself up, gripping the metal bars with both hands while the rope hung limply against the cage.

Quickly the countess reached through the bars, grasping Hugh's shoulders. With her help, he finally stood erect on the platform, running his hands through the bars for support.

"Mary Mother, I feared for you!" Countess Isabella gasped. "You are a brave man, Gordon of Glenbirnie, yet little more than a boy."

"For you I would dare greatly, Countess," Hugh said. "If you reach into the upper pocket of my tunic, you will find a link of gold chain from the king. It will identify me as the Bruce's agent."

"I do not have to look upon that gold, lad, but I will accept it as a token of the king's interest in my welfare," she said, plucking the link from Hugh's pocket. "The fact that you risked your life in this dangerous climb is evidence enough that you are the Bruce's faithful follower. What is your Christian name?"

"Hugh, Your Ladyship."

"A very fine name it is."

Hugh looked at the handsome woman with the glossy black hair turning to gray. The countess' face was pale as if she had not seen enough of the sun, but her eyes were alive, filled with a tensity of feeling which made Hugh realize the spirit of Isabella MacDuff, Countess of Buchan, was unconquerable.

"Your Ladyship," Hugh said. "The king sent you this message: He will try to storm Berwick Castle and rescue you in the near future. But first he must stamp out the

English strength in Galloway and break the power of the false MacDougalls of Lorn."

"Where is the Bruce now, Hugh, and is he well?"

"As well as could be expected, miladi, after being hunted for years by the English hounds the length and breadth of Scotland. His Highness defeated your husband, the Earl of Buchan, at Old Meldrum two weeks ago, sending the English forces reeling back to Aberdeen."

"That is indeed good news," said the countess. "Buchan's loss is Scotland's gain. He is a good hater, that husband of mine, a true Comyn. He has hated me ever since I placed the crown on Robert Bruce's head there at Scone. That was a long time ago."

"I have been sent to tell you of a possible attack on Berwick in the near future, Your Ladyship. As soon as the Bruce returns from the Western Isles, he can spare good fighting men for this venture in your behalf."

"This castle is wondrous strong," the countess said gravely. "And it cannot be taken without great loss of life, unless a surprise attack succeeds. I would not have good Scots killed so I could go free, young Gordon. Tell King Robert that."

"He intends to capture Berwick if he can, Countess, to rescue you and to strike the English a mortal blow. The fall of Berwick Castle would rally to his standard many Scots who are neutral."

"King Robert remembers his friends." The countess turned impulsively to Hugh. "And you are my friend, too, else you would not have made this perilous ascent of the wall to give me the Bruce's message. Tell me, what information about the castle do you desire?"

"Whatever you chance to hear, a word dropped here and there, miladi. Have the English treated you cruelly?"

"They are kind, compared to my husband, the traitor

Buchan. The governor of the castle is a crusty oaf, for all his high rank. Some of the younger officers come and talk to me through a grilled door at the other end of my prison. Men like Sir John Clifford."

"Is Sir John here?" Hugh asked. "I had dinner with him at Perth before he learned I was a king's man. A very courteous knight, it seemed to me."

"You are right, Hugh Gordon. Sir John is ever the gentleman. It is hard to remember he is English and an enemy of our country."

"Have you been able to learn the strength of the English garrison, miladi?"

"I would say that there are at least eight hundred behind these walls, some men-at-arms, but most of them archers. Strongly entrenched, they could keep at bay a much larger force of Scots. That is why I am reluctant to see the king undertake a siege of the place."

Hugh put his finger to his lips and they waited as a sentry passed on top of the wall, rattling his sword. "Of course, miladi, we could not hope to capture Berwick in an attack from the town side. Do you think Scots could scale this wall up which I climbed a few minutes ago?"

"It would be very difficult, unless all were young and active. Too many clutching hands would tear down this mantle of ivy. I think you would have to use ladders in a night attack."

"All of us would not have to climb to the top of the parapet, Countess. Just a few younger men like myself who could obtain a foothold on the wall and throw down ropes from hooks attached, like this one, to something substantial."

Isabella, Countess of Buchan, shook her head. "It seems to me a very dangerous task. But I am sure you and others like you will make the attempt, God help you!"

"I must leave now, miladi. My friend Angus waits for me in the skiff below."

Hugh kissed the countess' hand and knelt on the platform, feeling for the hook, securely held by the iron bar. "Your Ladyship, as soon as I reach the river below, I'll tug at the rope and you can release the rope and the hook, which will fall quietly into the water."

"Yes, lad. Be careful."

Slowly Hugh lowered himself beneath the level of the platform, winding his legs around the rope whose loose end disappeared into the darkness below. Steadily he went down, hand over hand, hoping Angus was near.

The rope burned his torn hands as it slithered through his fingers. It seemed as though his descent would never end when he heard Angus' voice from the darkness below. "Steady, lad, the skiff is under thee. About ten feet more."

Then he felt a powerful hand clutch at his thigh, guiding his feet down to the boat. Angus lowered him gently to the thwart, as the skiff rocked in the water. "You saw the countess, Hugh?"

"She is well, but not happy as a prisoner, of course. I gave her the king's message. Soon she will throw down the hook and rope."

"Good. If the hook splashes, the sentry will think it a fish. Even if it sinks like a stone before we can snatch the rope, it will have served us well. Move to the stern, lad."

They heard the hook hit the water, and Angus rowed swiftly toward the sound, but rope and hook had disappeared beneath the surface.

"No matter, saves us hauling it aboard. Now for the tavern, and a quick trip to Kelso in the early morning. When we reach our horses, we'll ride for Galloway. Does the idea please you?"

"Very much. I have been wondering, though, just how

our Scots can capture Berwick Castle. There is a wall around the town, and a stronger one around the castle."

"Did the countess know anything about the English forces in Berwick?"

"She estimates the troops in the castle at eight hundred. Behind those walls they can hold off a strong army."

"We will win our way inside the castle by ruse and trick, lad," Angus said confidently. "Let the Bruce and his leaders plan the attack. Our job is to let them know how many English they must meet in battle."

"I hope we can win this castle, Angus, and set the countess free."

"She is a MacDuff, lad, and the king will move heaven and earth to rescue her. You have already done your part, Hugh, and done it well."

The Walking Tower

It took three days' hard riding for Hugh and Angus to reach the king's headquarters at Ayr in Galloway. They had picked up their horses at Kelso and headed west in a hurry, staying close to the main road which angled west across central Scotland to Lanark and then dipped to the southwest.

Angus' gray and Sheila had kept pace, matching strides, as their riders gave them the spur. Occasionally they had had to hide out along the main road when troops of English cavalry passed by. But these interruptions were infrequent. As Angus put it, "We've pretty well cleaned the Saxons out of this part of Scotland."

Arriving at Ayr, Hugh and Angus had ridden directly to the house which the king was using as a headquarters. The Bruce was glad to see them, his face brightening as Hugh told about his talk with the countess. "You have done well, young man, and I commend thee for that dangerous climb to Isabella of Buchan's prison. Not many Scots could be that sure of foot in the dark, eh, Angus?"

"No, sire, certainly I could not have climbed that wall like a mountain goat."

The king stroked his yellow beard thoughtfully. "Young Gordon, could active Scots scale that battlement over-looking the river?"

"I am not sure, sire, but they could try. If a larger body were to stage an attack on the land side of Berwick Castle, it is possible the English would become so much inter-ested in defending that area that they would neglect the wall directly over the countess' prison."

"What think you, Angus?"

"I would say, Your Highness, that Hugh was right. But the attempt might fail, sire. One man, presumably Gordon here, would have to reach the top unnoticed, and haul up rope ladders. The first time Hugh climbed that wall, he was not burdened with targe and sword. And he was very fortunate, sire, to get as far as he did."

"I will have to think on this tonight," King Robert said. "But I am determined to attack Berwick. I shall consult Sir James Douglas, who is an expert at storming castles. The army is camped west of Ayr. Join it and wait for word from me. Again, my grateful thanks."

Hugh and Angus bowed out, then rode down the crooked streets of Ayr until they reached the countryside. There numerous fires gleamed across the great expanse of meadow, with the soldiers of the Bruce huddled close beside the flames in the chill March air.

Angus' gray picked its way unerringly through the camp to a fire surrounded by Highlanders in various tartans. "I think I will stay the night here, Hugh," Angus said. "You are welcome, although most of these men speak only the Gaelic."

"No, I'll ride on. I want to find Jock Lockhart, if I can. He may have word of my father and Glenbirnie."

"Let us meet in the morning at that tavern across the street from the king's headquarters. He will probably want to see us at some hour or other, and we will be close by."

"Agreed." Sheila tossed her head and pranced away through the dark, winding her way deftly through the maze of campfires. Finally Hugh found Jock bending over a skillet, intent on frying half a dozen eggs.

Hugh dismounted wearily. "That's a hearty meal, Jock, even for a Galloway man."

Lockhart started and turned around. "Hugh Gordon! You're just the Galloway man to help me eat it."

"Any hay for my Sheila, Jock?"

"Aye. The wagons unloaded big piles of it fifty yards due west of this campfire. Take Sheila over there and stake her out."

Hugh led the black mare into the darkness where a dozen horses were munching hay outside the ring of campfires. He took off Sheila's saddle and bridle, then attached her to the end of a long picket rope which he tied to a tree.

When he returned, Jock had a wooden plate and spoon ready for Hugh, the plate loaded with a favorite Scots dish, cubed fried potatoes and eggs. As Hugh finished the food on his plate, he looked up to see Jock looking intently at him across the fire, a sadness in his friendly eyes.

"Anything wrong, Jock?"

"No, lad, not with me. I—I—to tell you the truth, Hugh, I have bad news from Glenbirnie."

"Is it my father?"

"Aye, Hugh, he's been dead a month, God rest his soul."

"How did it happen, Jock?"

"Eh? Oh, very peaceful. The old gentleman just slept his life away one night. He had no pain, lad, and you should be thankful for it."

Hugh swallowed the lump in his throat. "Thank you, Jock. It is sad news. My heart will be heavy with sorrow this night. I suppose my precious cousin Alan is now lording it over Glenbirnie," he added dully.

"No, no, Hugh, that's what I'm coming to. The hand of God was in it, man. Thomas Dickson told me Alan was there at the funeral. When he started home, his horse slipped on the cobblestones in the castle yard and threw your cousin. He never became conscious again."

"I suppose I should be sorry for Alan's death, since he was my blood kin. But after the way he treated my father, I cannot grieve."

"No one has come forward to claim the property, lad," Jock said. "It is being cared for by Thomas Dickson who accepts rent money from the peasants. Old Thomas, I think, is honest and will keep your holding safe until you return."

"Aye, he's a fine man, Thomas." Hugh lay down on the ground. "Is this your blanket, Jock?"

"Keep it, lad, and sleep warm. Good night."

Hugh was awake for some time, crying in his heart, wishing that he could visit Glenbirnie again. But he knew the king planned an immediate attack on Berwick and realized the Bruce was depending heavily on him. His ability to scale the wall on the Tweed side of Berwick

Castle might well make the difference between victory and defeat for the Scots army.

At last he fell into a heavy sleep and woke early the next morning, cold and stiff. Hastily he walked over to the tree to which Sheila was tied, picking up the saddle and bridle hanging on a branch.

As the mare nuzzled him, he put his arms around her neck. "You're a Galloway horse, and I'm a Galloway man, and I wish we were both back at Glenbirnie, watching Jamie chase rabbits. It's all so long ago, Sheila, and so much has happened since we left home."

He saddled and bridled the mare, then rode back to Jock's fire where Lockhart was stretching and yawning, barely awake. "I'm to headquarters for the day, Jock. Many thanks for the meal and the bed."

"You're welcome as you can be, lad. Don't you want breakfast?"

"No, I should be on my way. I'll see you again, Jock."

When Hugh entered the presence of the Bruce next morning, he was deeply disappointed to hear his king announce the march on Berwick would be long delayed.

"I have talked to Sir James and he advises against immediate attack. There are so many strongholds still held by the English here. It desolates me to think of the Countess of Buchan held a prisoner, but Douglas feels the campaign would be a mistake."

"Yes, sire."

"Later, when we have strengthened our position in Scotland, Berwick will be our first concern."

Hugh left the king, sober-faced and heartsick. He knew he was too young to know what should be done, and when it should be done. All he could think about was the plight of Isabella of Buchan.

For the next three years, her face haunted him, as he

fought in dangerous night attacks and made swift forays with Douglas across the Border into England. Like Jock Lockhart and Angus Maclean, he became a highly trained soldier.

Occasionally he visited Glenbirnie Castle, fishing for salmon in Loch Urr and hunting the red deer in the hills. But always, he went back to the Bruce's army, waiting for the day when the king would order an attack on Berwick.

Hugh knew the countess was alive and in reasonably good health. But he thought often that she must have given up hope.

It was October, 1311, when Hugh hastened back to the Bruce after returning from a raid against the MacDougalls, English supporters in western Galloway. As he dismounted at the inn on Ayr's main street, Jock Lockhart beckoned him.

"The king intends to attack Berwick soon. You and Angus and I are going."

"I can't wait to start, Jock. It's been a long time. I'll get inside the castle or die!"

A week later an army of two thousand Scots, led by Sir James Douglas, stretched out on the road to Cummock, heading toward Berwick. The men were hard-bitten troops who had seen hard campaigning all over Scotland. They did not know where they were going, but the sight of Douglas in the lead put them in fine fettle. Where Sir James went, the fighting was thickest.

Hugh was one of a score of skirmishers trotting well in front of the army, watchfully looking over the road. Douglas had picked Hugh especially for the job of scout. "With eyes like yours," the swarthy Scots commander had said, "you should see halfway to Berwick."

Jock Lockhart was with the advance guard, too, glad of the chance to keep an eye on Hugh. Just behind the skirmishers rode fifty knights in full armor, with their men-at-arms following them. In the middle of the long column marched tall Highlanders, tough fighting men who had followed the Bruce to Ireland when his fortune was at a low ebb, and who were now with him in their native country, eager for victories.

Walking with giant stride at the head of the High-landers was Angus Maclean, a Lochaber ax on his right shoulder, a quiver of arrows on his back, a bow in his hand. Hugh had been reluctant to part company with Angus, but there was no choice; orders were orders. Hugh knew that when the army started to besiege Berwick he would see more of his friend.

The column swept past Lanark on the road to Kelso, moving slowly along the winding Tweed River. As the army approached Berwick, Hugh grew more cautious, occasionally waving Sir James to a stop, while his keen eyes searched every clump of bushes, and every heavily wooded glen, for a possible ambush.

As the Scots resumed the advance, Hugh touched Jock's arm. "We can't be too careful. If the English bowmen ever found our army drawn out in a long military formation, it would go hard with us."

"Stop worrying, man. This force is too big to conceal in a hay wagon. Unless the English are complete fools, they know already we are nigh Berwick."

Hugh groaned. "They may carry the countess deeper into England, to make sure they will not lose her as a hostage!"

"Knowing Englishmen, Hugh, I think not. If we banged on the gate of Berwick and demanded Isabella of Buchan, they would feel sure they could hold the place against ten thousand Scots. And that overconfidence might well mean defeat for them."

A bugler riding close to Sir James Douglas blew a sharp blast. At the signal, Hugh turned Sheila and galloped back to his leader.

Douglas' dark face was grim. "Gordon, how far to Berwick?"

"Around fifteen miles, sir. The road follows the Tweed all the way."

"Good. I think we will camp somewhere soon. The English will know we are approaching. I want the troops to move forward refreshed, after a good night's sleep. Do you know a good camping place?"

"Sir, Kelso is only three miles distant. There is a great meadow adjoining the village on the east."

"Good. We will camp there tonight."

Next morning the Scots pushed forward through the cold sunless day, filled with good food and rested after a long night's sleep. By noon, they crossed the Tweed and neared the walls of Berwick.

Sir James had ridden forward to join Hugh as they jogged steadily toward the great seaport town with its huge sprawling castle. Douglas set spurs to his horse and dashed ahead, with Hugh close behind. Suddenly he drew up. "The gates are shut, and there's no sign of life on the walls. Is there a moat ahead of us, Gordon? I haven't been to Berwick in years."

"Yes, sir, there is a moat. The bottom is muddy, but I would say men could cross it without sinking too deep."

"Good. We'll draw up the army in battle formation and out of arrow range. Then I want you to send Angus to me without delay. Get Lockhart to call up two companies of Galloway men. There's important work to do."

"Shall I go now, sir? You would be left alone."

Douglas smiled and slapped the flank of his big black

stallion. "If they sally forth, this fellow will show them a clean pair of heels. Be on your way, Gordon."

"Yes, sir."

Hugh returned to Sir James with Angus and Jock Lockhart. The Scots leader eyed the Maclean. "Those huts over there by the Tweed, do Scots or English live there?"

"Scots, Sir James. Fishermen, laborers, and artisans. Inside Berwick are the homes of the rich English merchants, and a few of our countrymen. The Scots over there by the river are loyal to the king."

"Good. Get over there and see if you can find a few carpenters. As you go, locate some timber, planks and the like. Bring back all the wood possible."

"Yes, Sir James."

As they neared the cottages on the riverbank, Angus explained to Hugh just what Douglas had in mind. "He's going to build a siege tower, lad, and try to 'walk it' up to the walls of Berwick. I have never seen one, but I hear Sir James has used them freely in attacks on English-held castles in Galloway."

By nightfall the entire Scots army was encamped on the plain, well back from Berwick's walls, with sentries posted to warn Douglas of a possible attack after nightfall. Behind the army the camp boiled with activity, carried on in the light of flaming torches. Carpenters were busy building a tower.

The base of the structure, as Hugh could see, consisted of four wooden wheels, two on each side. The floor of the movable fortress was twelve feet square. As the cross timbers rose in the air, Hugh watched the job of construction with intense curiosity, noting that at the top the tower would be barely eight feet across.

All night, and the following day, the carpenters worked hard, putting two-inch boards on the framework of the fortress, fastening bullhide shields to the boards, shields which could deflect the strongest arrow.

Hugh thought the tower finished, but still the men worked, adding what looked like a ten-foot drawbridge to the top. He turned to Angus in amazement. "What is that?"

Angus quit gnawing on a joint of lamb. "When we roll the tower across the moat and up to the wall of Berwick, the men inside the structure will let down the bridge. While our archers on the ground keep up a hot fire, our men-at-arms inside the tower will cross the bridge to the wall, leap down from the parapet, and attack the English.

"As you have perhaps noticed," Angus went on, "there is a trap door in the floor of the tower. Men pushing the tower closer to the wall can enter the structure, climb the ladders on the inside and pop out at the English from the top!"

"It sounds dangerous, Angus. The English bowmen will shower us with arrows and those arrows bite deep."

"All war is dangerous, lad. Our archers will be busy, too, filling the air with shafts around that drawbridge. I think I will be in the tower with my ax, but Sir James will not let you take the risk, Hugh. He will need you later, for the task of scaling that castle wall facing the Tweed."

Hugh was silent. More than ever, he realized that war meant death to many, friends as well as enemies. He could see clearly that Angus might be struck down, once he left the shelter of the tower and leaped out onto that drawbridge.

Three days later Sir James Douglas was ready for the attack. Slowly, steadily, the walking tower rolled forward on its ponderous wheels, nearing the wall around Berwick. Behind it trailed a company of Galloway men, shoving the structure ahead of them.

Angus, as he had predicted, was stationed inside the tower, along with Scots knights and men-at-arms in full armor, equipped with swords and axes. Hugh, riding with Sir James, was in a sober mood. He longed to be inside the tower with Angus. At the same time, he could not understand why Douglas was risking Angus' life as a soldier when the Highlander was so valuable as a spy.

Sir James seemed to read his thoughts. "Your friend Angus Maclean will be the first man on that drawbridge when it is let down on the wall. I selected him because he is as strong as a bull and deft with the Lochaber ax. A man like that, spearheading our attack, can mean the difference between success and failure."

It was dark as the tower moved toward the wall. English soldiers were now manning the flat roof behind the parapet, sending a stream of arrows against the tall, wooden structure, but their shafts glanced off its sides. Sir James shouted a command, and the Galloway men stopped pushing. Soon the entire Scots line had retreated out of arrow range, except for a few heavily armored knights clustered around the base of the tower.

"We'll attack at dawn," Sir James said. "Meanwhile, our foot soldiers and archers can get some sleep. The knights and men-at-arms around the tower can stay there all night, guarding it against a surprise attack from Berwick. There'll be little rest for those lads," he added grimly. "Nor for me."

Hugh slept heavily that night in the Scots camp, then awoke early and ran immediately to the tower, leaving Sheila behind. He found Jock Lockhart nearby the wooden fortress, weary and red-eyed from lack of rest. On the wall of Berwick, pine torches were still burning as the English kept watch.

Jock pointed to the wall. "The English have been up all night, thinking the tower would be moved forward any minute. Sir James figured they'd stay awake and be in poor shape to fight today. He was right. The enemy is not nearly as fresh as our army."

Just then Sir James in his black armor rode rapidly up to the tower and shouted to Jock. "We're moving forward at once. Be alert."

Hugh could hear the tread of Scots archers marching smartly forward toward the wall of Berwick. The bowmen would have the task of accompanying the tower on its trip to the wall, shooting at any English head which appeared above the parapet.

Meanwhile, Jock's Galloway men started to push hard against the back end of the tower. As the structure creaked slowly ahead, English bowmen filled the air with arrows. Hugh could see the missiles falling harmlessly off the sides of the tower, but they were beginning to cause trouble among the Scots archers, who wore leather shirts instead of armor. Now and then a man sagged to the ground, a shaft in his body, but his place was taken immediately by another.

As the wooden fortress moved forward, the Scots on the ground stepped aside and waited for the English to show themselves above the parapet. When they did, Douglas' bowmen sent flights of arrows winging to the wall as the tower kept walking steadily toward the moat, propelled forward by Jock Lockhart's sturdy Galloway men.

The tower finally reached the ditch and stopped, while Jock cautiously circled around to the front and inspected the ditch. He came racing back to cover, with English arrows whizzing dangerously close.

"There's no water in the moat, men," he shouted. "Bottom is full of rushes and reeds, a bit muddy, but passable. I think we can get it across. Forward!"

The Galloway men sweated and strained, shoving against the beams of the walking tower, which lurched down into the moat. Once the structure seemed to be mired down in the mud, but Jock's company heaved and lifted it forward, inching it up to the wall in spite of the English arrow hail.

Men down in the ditch, their footing in the mud uncertain, gave a last desperate heave, and the citadel constructed of scrap timber finally moved forward the last precious feet, so that the drawbridge could reach the wall.

Hugh ran back fifty feet and to the side, in order to watch the siege operation. By this time the arrow hail from the walls had ceased. English men-at-arms in mail had taken the place of bowmen, waiting grimly for the first occupant of the tower to cross that drawbridge. Looking at the English waiting there, Hugh's heart was heavy. The first man across the bridge and down into the ranks of the men-at-arms would probably never survive.

The door of the walking tower suddenly opened, and the drawbridge dropped down on top of the parapet. Out from the fortress stalked Angus Maclean. He stepped lightly across the bridge, his Lochaber ax ready in his hand.

One of the English men-at-arms climbed out onto the bridge from the parapet, swinging his sword. Giving his enemy the point of the ax, then swinging the blade, Angus knocked the Englishman off the drawbridge and down into the moat. A wild cheer rose from the Scots below as Angus leaped down off the drawbridge and inside the parapet, with half a dozen Scots from the tower following him.

Hugh could not now see Angus in action, but he knew that the big axman had probably secured a firm footing on the roof, because the drawbridge was still firmly in place, and more Scots were pouring across it to the para-

pet. They came rapidly up from the lower recesses of the
tower, rushing to the aid of Angus and those Scots who
had already climbed across the drawbridge to the wall
of Berwick.

The city's main gate was fifty feet south of the tower. In
front of the entrance, well back from arrow range, Sir
James Douglas with a hundred and fifty mounted knights
and men-at-arms sat waiting for the Scots on the wall to
fight their way to the main gate and drop the drawbridge
over the moat. Across that moat and in through that gate,
Douglas intended to lead a desperate charge.

It seemed hours to Hugh before the drawbridge started
to come down from the gate. Hugh knew it was being
lowered by the Scots who had cut their way down from
the wall. He wondered if Angus were still alive, still their
leader. There was no way of knowing.

Finally the bridge rattled to the ground, and a throaty
cheer rose from the Scots cavalry. Douglas raised his arm,
shouting "God and Saint Andrew!" Then the riders spurred
forward at a gallop, lances at rest, and swept inside the
gate, into the city of Berwick, with archers and spearmen
running after them on foot, all eager to close with the
enemy inside the walls.

Hugh was picked up and carried forward on a resistless
tide of yelling Scots, through the gate and into the city.
Gradually he worked his way to one side of the narrow
street choked with horses and men. He kept looking up at
the wall, looking for Angus. But the big Highlander was
nowhere to be seen. Was he dead? Hugh prayed to Saint
Columba for the safety of his friend.

Finally he ran up the steps leading to the flat roof to
which Angus had leaped from the drawbridge of the
tower. In a corner by the stone landing halfway to the
top, he found Angus. The Maclean's coat of mail was

badly dented, and a bloody bandage encircled his head.

"Angus! Angus!" Hugh shouted. "You are alive!"

"Barely so, lad," Angus said wearily. "I feel half dead, buffeted as I have been by the swords of the English." He glanced down at the coat of mail. " 'Tis good protection, but inside the links, I am black and blue. Every time I felt a sword stroke, I wondered if the blade would cut all the way to my skin."

"I'll get you back to camp, Angus," Hugh said. "Our entire army is now inside the town, fighting its way toward Berwick Castle. But I'm not supposed to take part in the battle, since I must lead the attack on the river side of the castle later."

"Then what are you doing here, lad? Let us be going while my legs can still hold me up."

Angus rose slowly to his feet, using the broken haft of his ax as a cane. With his arm around Hugh's shoulders, he went slowly down the steps and toward the main gate.

As they walked across the drawbridge, Hugh heard, ringing in his ears, the shouts of the Scots driving hard against the English inside Berwick, "God and Saint Andrew! A Douglas! A Douglas!"

Angus smiled grimly. "The Border clans make a mighty noise, Hugh, you can hear an angry Scot a mile away. The countess must know we are here, lad."

Ladders in the Dark

After two days of house-to-house fighting, the army of Douglas drove what was left of the English garrison into Berwick Castle. The walls of the fortress were almost twice as high as those which surrounded the town itself, and the siege came suddenly to a halt while Sir James talked to carpenters and artisans.

Many of the Scots in Berwick had been shipbuilders. They were thoroughly familiar with the work. But as one grizzled old man told Douglas, "It will take time, Your Lordship."

The black Douglas scowled, but his voice was gentle. "How much time, old man?"

"Two weeks, perchance."

Hugh, standing close by, saw Sir James' face darken.

"We can't wait that long," he explained curtly. "By this time Sir Guy Warren, the governor of Berwick, has no doubt dispatched a fast sloop southward to an English east coast port, asking for aid. We will build scaling ladders, soundly constructed of wood. At least that can be done quickly."

The conference was still going on when Hugh mounted Sheila and rode back to the camp outside the walls, where some Scots remained, to watch the road from England for possible reinforcements moving up to assist the hard-pressed garrison of Berwick Castle.

He found Angus sitting lazily with his back against a small larch tree, sniffing the stew bubbling in the pot before him. The big man waved a greeting. "Sit down, man, dinner is almost ready."

"I've eaten, Angus. How do you feel today?"

"Strong as a Highland bull, lad. I have taken off the bandage, as you can see. The doctor swears I'm well. He says no English sword ever made could split my thick skull."

"I'm not so sure of that. I remember how I felt after Glen Trool. My head rang for days. By the way, Angus, Sir James says you have done your work here by breaching the wall. Others are to carry the fight at the front gates of the castle."

Angus was plainly annoyed. "How about our attack on Tweedside, the scaling of the castle wall at night? I will be there, lad, if only to give you a boost up to the ivy."

Hugh was touched. "We could not climb that wall without your help. But you will stay at the bottom of the wall, to fish out of the river any unfortunate who misses his footing on the rope ladders."

"That I will do, lad. In the Highlands, I'm famous as a fisherman. Mostly salmon," Angus said, with a twinkle in his eyes. "I'll rescue any Scot who ducks himself into the Tweed."

For four days and nights the local carpenters, assisted by some of the Galloway Scots, built wooden ladders thirty feet high, tapering to a narrow top. The walking tower Douglas had used to conquer the town wall was too big to be taken inside the main gate.

"I'd tear it down and use the wood for another, but there wouldn't be time. We'll just have to do with what we've got." Sir James looked at Hugh. "Gordon, your attack will be the important one. We will hold the garrison while you sneak up on their rear. Good hunting!"

Two nights later, skiffs with muffled oars landed two hundred carefully picked Scots at the foot of the castle wall which overlooked the Tweed. On a ledge about six feet wide which ran around the base of the wall, Hugh and his men relaxed before the attack.

Black Angus, who accompanied the expedition as observer and organizer, was encased to his knees in a coat of mail. In his belt he had thrust a sword, in a stocking beneath the Maclean kilt was a sharp dirk.

Hugh whispered to Angus, "Yon moon will go under a cloud soon. When we hear the noise of the fight at the front gate, I'm hoping the sentries above us will be anxious to engage in it and will desert their posts."

"I haven't heard a sound from the wall, not a sound," Angus said.

Hugh glanced up, straining his keen eyes. Although the Countess of Buchan's cage was only fifty feet from the ledge where he was resting, there was no sign of light. The evening was chill, and the countess had apparently retired for the night. "I'm glad she's inside, Angus."

Angus squinted into the dark. "I think you're right, lad. Now, let's plan the attack." He turned to the leader of

the Galloway men who had been chosen for the dangerous
mission. "Hugh will climb up the ivy and reach the top
of the wall, and we must give him plenty of time. He'll
have an iron hook stuck in his belt, with a rope trailing
behind. As soon as he reaches the parapet, he'll attach the
hook to a pillar, or something immovable, and tug on the
rope to attract our attention. Is it understood?"

"Aye, Angus," said the Galloway officer. "Someone
below will catch the loose end of the rope and attach to
it a rope ladder, which Hugh will haul up and anchor to
the parapet."

"Yes," Hugh said. "Then I'll throw the rope down again
to haul up another ladder, then another, until there are
eight in place."

"That's right, lad," Black Angus said. "By that time,
God willing, there will be plenty of Scots beside you on
the flat roof back of the parapet, all ready to rush on the
English from the rear. I think it will work, Hugh."

An hour later, the Galloway men knelt beside the
river, ready for the attack. Most of them were dressed in
light mail and were bearing swords. There were a few
bowmen, too, all ready and anxious for the fight to begin.
There was no sound but the quiet murmur of the Tweed,
for the Galloway captain had savagely impressed on his
soldiers the need for silence.

Hugh whispered to Angus, "Haven't heard a sound from
the castle. I wonder when Sir James will begin his battle
at the front gate."

No sooner had he spoken than a series of wild yells
rent the air from a distance. On the night breeze, the
sounds of conflict carried far, the noise of scaling ladders,
of clatter of sword on shield. Hugh could hear men running hard on the wall beside the parapet overlooking the
river.

"See, lad," Angus said. "The English from all parts of the castle are rallying at what they think is the chief point of danger, the front gate. They are confident their rear is secure. It's time to be up with you, lad." Angus lifted the hook over Hugh's belt. "God guard you, boy."

Standing on the big man's shoulders, Hugh searched through the ivy for a projecting stone and found it. Clutching the vines with one hand and the stone with the other, he pulled himself four feet above Angus' head. Holding to the wall at that point, he reached higher for another stone. Again he pulled himself laboriously toward the top.

His climb was more difficult than it had been on that other night when he had reached the cage of the countess. Now he was burdened with war gear, his coat of mail and sword. He had to move more slowly, yet there was a great need for speed. The English at the main gate might suspect a feint and come pelting back to the wall above.

Slowly, steadily, he made his way up, praying to Saint Andrew as he reached for the familiar projecting stones which were hidden in the ivy. He was now within a few feet of the top and paused to listen. There was not a sound from above, so he increased his speed. Finally he was within a few inches. He reached up and caught the edge of the parapet, then pulled himself up toward the heavy railing, wiggling his way through stone slabs which protected the dwarf wall at the top.

Puffing like a man who has run several miles, he hauled himself up and reached around to pull the hook from his belt. At a slight noise he crouched for a moment in the shadow of the iron and stone railing. But only the wind came to find him. Quickly he slipped the hook over the iron railing and then cast the rope down below.

In a few seconds, he felt a tug and hauled the rope

back up. A rope ladder came into view, a hook hanging from one end. Quickly he put the hook around the iron railing and shook the rope ladder to attract attention below. Then he let down his own rope again, and it soon brought up a second rope ladder, then another and another.

His arms ached, and his hands were sore. He was worn out, but he doggedly went on hauling up the rope ladders, knowing that he worked against time. Up and over, up and over, up and over.

He heard a slight sound below the parapet. Looking down, he could see Scots clustered around the first rope ladder, waiting for the word to climb. They came up to the top of the wall, the last man lowering the ladder again while the rest crouched in the shadow of the railing, waiting patiently for word from their leader.

Their officer, a tall, thin-faced officer with a steel headpiece in his bonnet, looked around impatiently as Hugh sent another rope below. "Hurry, Gordon. The time is growing short."

"I know, sir, but the noise at the front gate is dying down. I had hoped to get more men up here—"

"We have enough to start the attack. The rest can follow, as soon as they reach the top."

Even as he spoke, Hugh caught the glimmer of pine torches, carried by men running around the castle tower to the parapet alongside the Tweed.

"There they are, men," the Galloway officer shouted at the top of his voice. "Follow me!"

With Hugh at his side, he dashed across the flat roof, diving headlong into an English man-at-arms who swung an ax murderously in his direction. The Galloway officer swerved sideways, and the Englishman missed his stroke.

Hugh brought his heavy sword down hard on the man's helmet and he collapsed on the stone floor.

"Up the Douglas!" Hugh shouted. "Up the Douglas!" the Galloway men yelled as they clashed furiously with the Englishmen on the roof, with Hugh in the forefront of the battle, his big blade flashing in the moonlight, back and forth, back and forth.

From bowmen standing behind the English men-at-arms there came a flash of arrows. Many of the shafts went home, and the Scots staggered and fell, their leader along with a dozen others. Behind the archers, Hugh could see massed spearmen marching forward. "St. George for England!"

Steadily, with massive discipline, the English moved forward, stepping over fallen men, and their chant grew louder and louder. Hugh quickly glanced around toward the parapet behind him. Scots were still climbing over the railing, but they were few in number. His reinforcements were not moving up fast enough. It was obvious that the Scots inside the wall would have to go on the defensive.

He rushed forward into the front line of Scots, shouting "A Douglas! A Douglas!" and always his sword swung to and fro. The Galloway men surged after him, closing with the English men-at-arms. Their furious swordplay sent the first rank of the enemy reeling back, but the English spearmen brought them up short. With the men in the front rank kneeling and the spears of the second rank projecting forward, the English line resembled the back of a huge porcupine.

Hugh slashed savagely at the haft of one spear, cutting off the point, but another quickly took the place of the broken weapon as another spearman moved up to keep the formation intact. The English archers had retired behind their spearmen and began to draw their longbows, shooting at a close range into the ranks of the Scots.

Gradually, relentlessly, the English forced Hugh and his men back with sheer weight of numbers. By now Hugh had lost all track of time. He was bleeding from a long gash which ran from the nosepiece of his helmet to the edge of the chin. His body was sore from constant blows. He had narrowly missed death at the hands of an English spearman. Still he doggedly fought on, his mind numbed by battle.

The Scots were now giving way sullenly, retreating toward the rope ladders. The battle on the stone roof still raged, but the line of the attackers had been broken by the massed charge of the English. More of them were arriving all the time on the wall above the river. Hugh, trying to rally his men, again shouted "A Douglas," but his voice was only a hoarse whisper.

Out of the corner of his eye, he could see some of the Scots climbing over the parapet and taking to the ladders in hasty flight. He balanced wearily for a moment on the balls of his feet, then picked up a shield from the inert body of an English soldier.

Directly behind him, Hugh saw the pavement on the roof of the wall narrow to a width of six feet with a stone railing on each side. The English, pursuing, would have to cross that strip of stone which was protected on the one side by the parapet and on the other by an iron railing which overlooked the courtyard below.

He came to a sudden decision. He would hold that piece of pavement until he could fight no longer. The last Scot had retreated now across the strip and the English were advancing, half a dozen men-at-arms leading the attack.

Summoning all his strength, Hugh charged directly toward the nearest Englishman. He feinted with his blade, then brought it crashing down on the man's headpiece. As another soldier rushed him from the side, he whirled and backed up against the parapet, his blade flickering out to meet the Englishman's sword. He beat down the weapon, then aimed a blow at the throat. The Englishman fell, but another immediately took his place.

Hugh fought now like a man in a gray fog while the English swords beat a tattoo on his heavy shield. He stumbled, finished one sword stroke, then straightened up for another. An axman, rushing at him, struck his helmet a paralyzing blow which stretched him motionless on the stone pavement.

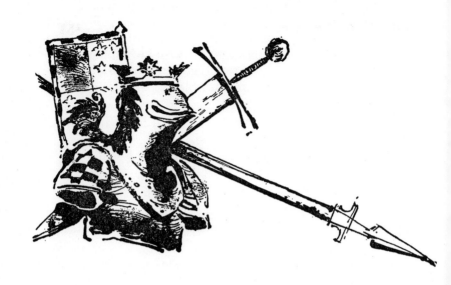

The Dungeon of Roslin

Hugh never knew when he first regained consciousness. He found himself lying flat on his back, his eyes and forehead bandaged. His first sensation was one of smell. The room or cell in which he was located seemed damp. There was a chill gust of air coming from some opening high above him. He suspected it was a small barred window high up in the wall.

Feebly he reached up and touched the bandage over his eyes, then ran his hand over the narrow pallet where he lay and felt straw. With fear that almost turned to panic, he realized that his eyesight might be gone. With aching head and stiff body, he cautiously moved first his arms, then his legs. At least he was not crippled.

He knew he was a prisoner somewhere in Berwick Castle, but he did not know how long he had been in the cell. Someone had bandaged his head. Judging from the weakness of his body, he knew he had lost a great deal of blood. That blow on his head indeed must have come close to killing him.

He wondered how long he had been out of his senses. He wondered what the English had in store for him, a Scot, a rebel. He was not really important enough to kill. He had given the English plenty of trouble but, as a prisoner, he was not a great prize, to be executed or ransomed for a large sum of money.

He supposed that the Scots had retreated after their failure to take the castle. Angus Maclean, he hoped, had survived, also Sir James Douglas. Hugh thought of the Countess of Buchan. He could do nothing for her now as she sat in prison, waiting vainly for rescue. She must have heard the clash of arms as the Scots attacked Berwick Castle, the war cries, the sound of desperate men in battle. Surely she must have felt freedom within her grasp, only to have it snatched away.

Someone was turning a key in the rusty lock, and he sensed a stranger entering his cell. He could not even see his visitor. It was as though a dark curtain had been drawn between him and the rest of the world. He was helpless if the newcomer intended to injure him. Never before had he realized how important clear vision was. Until now, he had been able to see like a hawk, a quality invaluable to King Robert. But that terrific blow in battle had changed everything. Now he could only wait and listen.

He lay quiet and tense, knowing the visitor was bending over his pallet. A cool hand touched his cheek, a friendly touch, like a hand held out to a child in the dark. "I am

Father Henry, my son, chaplain of the castle. How do you feel today?"

"I have a bad headache, Father, but that does not worry me. It is my eyes. Do you think I will ever see again?"

"We cannot tell as yet, my son. You took a hard knock on the head and bled freely from a cut over your eyes. The leech attended you earlier. He thinks it will be several weeks before we know if your sight will again be normal. Your eyes are in the hands of God."

The priest sat down on the pallet beside Hugh and took his hand. The young Scot's fingers closed convulsively, his voice a faint whisper. "To lose your eyes is to be like one dead, Father. There is nothing left."

The priest spoke gently but sternly. "That is an evil thought. You are alive, thanks to the leech's care. I have prayed for you daily, although you are a Scot and I am English. That I was glad to do, for are we not all God's children?"

"You are right, Father. I am grateful to God and Saint Andrew that I am still alive. And for your gentle care, my thanks. I am called Hugh Gordon."

"Yes, I know. You have a friend in Sir John Clifford. He has visited this room almost every day. As for the eyes, you must try to be patient. In God's good time you will, I hope, see again."

A rough voice interrupted the priest. "Father, I have to lock the cell again. You've done all you can for this one. He's a Scot, and born to be hanged."

"Be quiet, varlet, and look to your immortal soul!" Father Henry touched Hugh's arm. "I must go now, but I will return. Remember, my son, you are alive, and young."

Hugh, his sense of hearing more acute because of his

lost eyesight, heard the faint clink of spurs on the stone
floor of the corridor outside his cell. Then a familiar voice
spoke to the turnkey. "I would visit our Scots prisoner,
jailer, and here's a gold piece for your trouble."

Hugh tried to sit up but fell back, weak and helpless.
He heard Sir John greet the priest cordially and felt the
knight's hand on his shoulder. "Lie quiet, Gordon of
Glenbirnie. I see you have been at your good works again,
Father."

"That I have, Sir John. I hope I have given your young
friend some good advice. He worries overmuch."

"Faith, and I can't blame him."

"He has much to be thankful for, Sir John. I know how
you stayed an English sword about to slay young Gordon
on the wall of the castle. It was a deed of Christian char-
ity, my son."

Hugh reached for Clifford's hand. "I thank you with all
my heart, Sir John. I will obey the good father and try to
be patient. Tell me, did your act of mercy toward me get
you in trouble with your superiors?"

Sir John laughed lightly. "As a matter of fact, it did,
Hugh Gordon. But I told the governor of the castle, Sir
Guy Warren, that you were of gentle blood and had been
led into the Scots rebellion by overzealous friends. I hope,
Father Henry, that I may be forgiven a statement a little
short of the truth."

" 'Twas a small sin, Sir John. Had you told the governor
that this lad was a close friend and follower of Robert
Bruce, it might have gone hard with him. I leave you to
your talk, Sir John. Rest easy, young Gordon, in God's
name."

Hugh listened to the priest's retreating footsteps. "Are
we alone, Sir John?"

"Aye, lad. The turnkey, sullen dog that he is, has slipped out for a pint of ale."

"I know our attack on Berwick Castle failed. Tell me what happened."

"Few Scots were left alive on the wall after you fell, lad," Clifford said soberly. "Our men cut the rope ladders when some of your friends were halfway down, and they fell into the river. At the main gate, Douglas made little headway. His archers annoyed us a bit, but he could not get his scaling ladders into position. One or two Scots reached the top of the wall, no more."

Hugh's head ached dully as he listened to his friend's dismal tale.

"You know, my friend," Clifford said, "we would not have thought of that wall overlooking the Tweed, if some of the sentries posted there had not rushed down to see what was happening at the gate. An officer recognized them. Realizing they had left the wall unguarded, he warned the governor, who rushed a strong party of our soldiers to the parapet. You know the rest."

"And that is the way battles are won—and lost," Hugh said bitterly. "If that officer had not seen those sentries who had deserted their posts, we Scots might well have won our way into the castle."

"The fortunes of war, Hugh. If the sentries had not been drawn away by the clamor at the gate, they might have seen your men before they had finished their climb and killed them all. By the way, who was the first Scot over the parapet?"

"I was, sir."

"A daring feat, lad. I am glad the governor does not know that, else he would have had you hanged days ago."

"Sir John," Hugh said, "I was here at Berwick three years ago, and I scaled the wall to talk to the Countess of

Buchan. She said you had been very kind to her, and I assume you are still her friend."

"The countess is a brave and beautiful lady with the kind of valor any man would admire. So you scouted the castle and climbed up to her prison, eh? A rash and dangerous act, lad. But I have news for you. In a week or so, we will know whether or not you can travel. If you can, I go with you. The governor will be sending you to Roslin Castle near Edinburgh, where several Scots leaders are held captive. Since Sir Guy wants to get rid of me, I have been assigned to Roslin Castle as second in command of the English garrison there."

"I hope I can make that trip, Sir John." Hugh tried to keep his voice steady. "With my eyes as they were before."

"You will, lad. Now I go so you may rest. Until tomorrow."

The Englishman left, and Hugh, lying on the pallet, realized the iron door had not swung shut. Without eyes, he thought helplessly, he could not leave his prison. He was as secure as if he had been trussed up like a fowl.

A few minutes later, the turnkey came with an ill-smelling bowl of soup. It was poor eating, and part of the liquid was spilled down his front. In a thoroughly bad humor, he threw the bowl on the floor and turned his face to the wall, miserable with despair.

The days passed slowly, the long hours between dawn and night lightened by the visits of Sir John and Father Henry. Occasionally the leech inspected Hugh's bandages, a man with a gruff voice but unusually gentle hands.

"You're lucky, lad, that your head is so hard," the physician said. "That blow would have killed a softer man." Slowly he unwrapped the bandage on the Scot's forehead. "You have here a scar you will carry through life."

Hugh tapped the bandage the leech had failed to re-

move from his eyes. "Will I see again, tell me?" His voice
was high-pitched, almost shrill with fear.

The leech paused a long time. "I am a physician, Scot,
no more. I merely do the best I can. Come Saturday, I
will take off the bandage."

The next few days dragged slowly, the minutes like
hours. No dawn or sunset separated the night from the
day for one who could not see. He remembered the blind
men of Galloway who sat motionless in the sun all day.
They could not see the smoke rising from the chimneys of
Douglaston. They could not see the swift hawk winging
his way across the hills. They could not see the blue sheen
of Loch Urr's waters. They were like old hounds waiting
to die.

Was that what the future held for him? Was he doomed
never to see the hills and woodlands, the winding river
and the open sea? Helplessly, with long dry sobs, he
beat his fists against the damp stones of his cell, alone
and without hope.

Then he felt his hands inspecting the wall, as though
his long, sensitive fingers were his eyes. He touched the
rivulets of water, the bits of moss, the stones fitted so
skillfully together. He listened carefully and could sepa-
rate the steps of his various guards as they moved down
the corridor past his cell. He could identify the greasy
beef soup long before the bowl was thrust into his hands.
The cook had added more meat today. He could taste it.

Slowly but surely a faint spark of hope grew. Since he
could not see, his other senses had been sharpened. Perhaps they would become even more highly developed. If
he tried, he might even ride again. Perhaps he could still
be useful to Scotland's king and Scotland's cause. No,
never would he sit in the sun, with folded hands!

He remembered again Father Henry's words. *You are*

fortunate to be alive. Your eyes are in God's hands. Quietly
Hugh recited the prayers the monks at St. Cuthbert's had
taught him, prayers he had almost forgotten.

Finally the key grated in the lock, and he heard the
leech's voice. "Lad, we are here to take a look at those
eyes. Father Henry is with me, also Sir John."

The priest patted Hugh's shoulder. "I hope my prayers
have been answered, young Gordon."

"Thank you, Father."

The leech deftly unwound the bandage, removing the
last fold from Hugh's eyes. For a second, Hugh lay
silent and shaken. Like a man making a far journey, he
finally opened his eyes, to see Sir John's familiar face.

"I can see! I can see!" he shouted, grasping Clifford's
outstretched hand. "Father Henry, your prayers have
been answered!"

"I am happy, lad, so happy," Sir John said. "All is well,
and soon we will be on our way to Roslin—together."

The leech and Father Henry left the cell, but Sir John
stayed. "I tried to get you better quarters, Hugh, but I
am not on good terms with the governor. However, I did
talk to the countess, who has been worried about you. She
will be wondrous glad when she learns you have regained
your sight."

"Poor lady," Hugh said. "I am sorry we Scots failed her
so miserably."

"The Countess Isabella does not blame you. She will
be happy that you are well again. I'll see if I can take you
to her for a farewell before we leave tomorrow morning."

Before dawn Hugh was up and nervously pacing his
cell. Sir John had loaned him fresh apparel which made
him feel almost human again. He was still a prisoner, to
be sure, but he was being taken to Roslin Castle—in
Scotland. There was always a chance that Sir James

Douglas or some other Scots leader would find the key to unlock the door of his new prison.

When Sir John came to escort him through the court-yard and up the winding stairs to the countess' heavily barred door, Hugh realized his imprisonment had been short compared to that of Isabella of Buchan.

However, as he kissed the hand the countess extended through the bars of her prison, he knew from her face that she was not bitter.

"It has been a long time, miladi, since I climbed the wall to your prison. I am sorry we could not attack Berwick earlier, but King Robert could not muster enough strength. I hope you understand."

"Of course I understand. I regret that you were captured, Hugh Gordon, but happy your eyes are sound again. Only one thing I regret, that so many brave Scots died here at Berwick trying to win my freedom."

"For you, Countess, they were glad to give their lives. All Scotland knows of Your Ladyship's heroism and self-sacrifice. I am a prisoner, and I do not regret it. At least I had a chance to fight for you."

Countess Isabella smiled as she turned to Sir John. "You have been a true friend, indeed. You told me Hugh Gordon was to be taken to another English prison here in Scotland, and I will not ask where, since I know you cannot tell me. But my best wishes and prayers go with both of you. Will you return to Berwick, Sir John?"

"No, miladi. I am under orders to join the garrison at the castle where Gordon will be held prisoner. I am only glad I could make your life more pleasant while I was stationed here."

"I will miss you," the countess said, "for there are few others here who will be as kind as you have been. They will make me feel like an enemy rather than a friend."

"You could never be my enemy, Countess."

Hugh and Sir John bade Isabella of Buchan farewell and descended the narrow stairway to the courtyard where a beefy English sergeant held a big bay for Hugh to mount.

As he felt a horse between his knees again for the first time in many weeks, he wondered what had happened to Sheila. Probably he would never see the faithful little mare again, or Jock, or Angus, or the men who had followed him up the rope ladders of Berwick.

They rode away into the May sunshine with Hugh taking not a backward glance at the place which held so many painful memories. He knew he had fought the best he knew how there on the stone pavement above the Tweed. But Sir James Douglas had not been there to see what happened. Perhaps Sir James would feel he had not done his best for the Bruce.

All the way to his new prison Hugh was a victim of his own gloomy thoughts. Nor could Sir John rouse him by pointing out the beauties of the countryside as the English detachment rode through the Lammermuir hills on the road to Roslin Castle.

"Have you ever been at Roslin, Hugh?" Sir John asked.

Hugh tried to be courteous. "No sir, but I know it is near the Firth of Forth."

"The castle is situated on a vast plain surrounded by some very fertile farmland. Since it is now a prison for highborn Scots, you will no doubt find friends there."

"I do not think so, Sir John. I am new to the king's army and I am sure most of the nobles and leaders now in prison were captured long ago."

When Hugh first saw the huge bulk of Roslin Castle rising in the distance, he was sick at heart. It did not look like an easy castle to capture. And here there would be no kindly priest to make his life more bearable. Nor could he endanger Sir Clifford's position by accepting favors from him.

"Sir John," Hugh said quietly, "when we arrive, it may be best for you to conceal the fact that we have been friends. Your new commander might not approve."

"I like whom I please," Sir John said stiffly.

"I appreciate your kindness, but you have a career at stake in the English army. I would not have you do aught to harm your rank."

"We shall see, Hugh. I will sound out the new commander and see how big his bite is. But, however the die is cast, I shall be able to do you a few favors. A turnkey can always be bribed to carry a well-cooked meal to a prisoner. At least I can see to it that you eat well."

As they rode across the moat and through the huge gate of Roslin Castle, servants rushed to hold the mounts. The men-at-arms dismounted stiffly and led their horses back to the stables for a rubdown and a half bushel of oats.

Sir John nodded to a tall English bowman. "Archer, here is a new Scots prisoner to be placed with the others." He turned to Hugh with a show of formality. "You will find your accommodations most sound. There is no chance of escape. I will announce your arrival to the governor."

The archer in Lincoln green touched Hugh's shoulder. "You will follow me, sir."

The Englishman took Hugh down a dark passage, rousing a turnkey who unlocked a large iron door at the end of the corridor.

Three men stood up in the half-light of the oblong cell. He recognized Lord Colin Kennedy, a Galloway man, and met Alan MacIver, a hawk-nosed Highlander from the Western Isles who lay on a couch, his eyes bright with fever. The other two prisoners were knights, men who showed the signs of long imprisonment.

Hugh settled easily into the life of the dungeon, for it was much the same as he had endured before. He did not complain of the poor food or the straw pallets on the stone floor. After all, his cellmates had eaten and slept in such fashion much longer than he had.

Lord Kennedy told him the others had given up hope. "But a Galloway man never stops hoping," he added. "We know that sooner or later Sir James Douglas will come tramping through the heather to our aid. It may be a long time, but he will come."

The pleasant month of June melted into the heat of July, then August. Hugh tried not to think too much about an attack on Roslin which would free him; yet, like Lord Kennedy, he refused to believe that help would never come.

The days were long and hot and monotonous except when an abundant meal appeared miraculously and even MacIver stirred from his couch to feast with the rest.

"I wonder what good angel has taken pity on us," Kennedy mused. "This beef is wonderfully cooked."

Hugh said nothing, for he was not sure his new-found friends would understand Sir John's generosity. If they knew about it, they might even feel Hugh was a spy, introduced into their prison to obtain information.

Even Sir John sensed the danger of the situation and on his few trips of inspection through the dungeon treated Hugh with the same formal courtesy he gave to the others.

One day the shuffling turnkey opened the door of the cell and bawled Hugh Gordon's name at the top of his voice. Hugh scarcely knew what to expect. Perhaps he was to be hanged after all. It was with relief he found himself turned over to Sir John on the flat stone roof of the outer castle wall.

Sir John waited until the bribed turnkey had disappeared. "I prevailed on the governor to let you out for an hour or so. Told him I was trying to get from you the campaign plans of Bruce's army. I assume you have such plans conveniently stowed away in your head!"

Hugh smiled. "No, Sir John, but right glad I am for a breath of fresh air and a glimpse of the sky and countryside."

"I must get back to the governor's office. As you can see, most of our men are out haying, bringing in provision for our horses in the winter months to come. We do not have many men in the garrison right now. I am glad your Sir James Douglas and his soldiers do not know how weak we actually are. But I scarcely think you can shout that information to him from this distance."

Sir John turned to go. "I'll tell the turnkey to put you back in your cell in half an hour. It's not much, but the best I can manage, Hugh."

"My thanks for those good meals, Sir John. I speak for all my friends who if they knew you were their benefactor would regard you as one of God's angels."

Sir John smiled. "I do not think I fit that role, but I accept the compliment."

Hugh watched his English friend leave and turned back to the parapet, drinking in the sweet, fresh air and feeling the warm sun on his prison-white face. He could see the members of the garrison raking hay in a field half a mile from the castle. He blamed them little for taking their time and lazing in the warm meadow. Many of them, he realized, were country boys accustomed to rural life just as he was.

He looked at them with envy for a few moments, then

turned and stretched his shoulders, sniffing the cool breeze which had begun to blow from the Firth of Forth. He leaned on the parapet looking down at the main gate of Roslin, noticing that several huge wagons were rolling out from the courtyard to carry back the hay raked in the distant field.

He followed the wagons with his eyes, wishing he were riding past the cool green trees at the side of the road and heading into the new-raked meadow. As the empty cart headed toward the hay rakers, another wagon came from behind the trees and set out for the castle. Hugh was puzzled. The wagon looked like any other, but the driver surely had not had time enough to load the wagon and start back. Probably two wagons worked in relays.

He shrugged and watched as the loaded van came closer, rolling across the drawbridge over the moat and into the entrance of the gate. Suddenly the driver pulled the horses at right angles and blocked the drive. A man jumped out with a sharp ax and cut the ropes used to raise the drawbridge.

Out of the wagon tumbled eight more heavily armed men. Hugh, with his hopes soaring, recognized the first man with the ax—Angus Maclean!

The burly Highlander dived into the gateway, backed by seven of his countrymen. Hugh lost sight of them now, but he could hear the roar of battle, the savage clash of arms, and the familiar cry of the Maclean clan, *"Bas no Beatha!"*

He started to run down to the gate, but stopped. He knew he was helpless without a weapon. From what he could see of the courtyard, the few English soldiers left in the castle were divided and confused. He heard Sir John rush out and rally his men.

Hugh had no way of knowing how many men Sir John

could muster, but it would be more than eight Scots could overpower, once the element of surprise had faded.

Then to his amazement a wild chorus of cries came from outside the castle. As if springing from the earth, hundreds of Scots archers and spearmen burst from the wood and headed for the castle. Led by mounted knights, they swept through the gate in waves of fury to relieve Angus and his handful of men.

Hugh could stand it no longer. Fight he would, if only with his bare hands! He dashed headlong to the inside stairway leading down to the great hall just as the turnkey came into view. Leaping on the man with all his weight, he gave the fat jailer a cuff on the ear and brushed past him.

He knew he must find a weapon somewhere if he was to help Angus. Quickly his eyes darted around the hall. Just off the big room he could see two offices. One must be that of the governor and the other would belong to Sir John. He bolted across the room and ran into the largest office. Luck was with him. The governor, overseeing the haying, had left his sword on the oaken table.

Hugh snatched up the weapon as he ran, buckling on the belt and feeling again the honest hardness of steel beneath his eager hand. He slowed his pace now and rounded the corner of the great hall where he could take a quick look at the fighting before flinging himself into the battle.

A sudden rush of attackers had split the ranks of the defending Englishmen. A wave of Scots had already engulfed the men-at-arms fighting beside Sir John. The Englishman was backing up the stairs of the castle alone, faced by Angus Maclean and his axmen.

Hugh saw it all at a glance and knew what he had to do. Carefully he crept down the stairs from the main hall to the courtyard, pausing just to the rear and slightly to the

right of the hard-pressed English knight who had befriended him. His borrowed sword snaked out and sent
Sir John's blade clattering down the steps.

Sir John turned in anger and Angus Maclean raised his
ax for the kill.

"My prisoner, Angus, stay your ax!" shouted Hugh.

The Highlander, bewildered, lowered his ax and wiped
the sweat from his eyes. Then he saw Hugh and his big
face broke into a smile of relief. "So, Galloway man, you
are back with us. *Cead mille failte*—a hundred thousand
welcomes!"

"Thanks, Angus." Hugh turned to Sir John, whose face
was white and set. "It was the only way, the only way to
disarm you in time to save your life. If I have offended
you, I crave pardon. I would not have you slaughtered
even by my best friend. You did as much for me, if you
remember."

Sir John regained his cheerful courtesy. "So I did,
Gordon, and I thank you for your generosity. The tables
are turned now. By fortune of war I am now your prisoner."

Seeing that Angus looked puzzled, Hugh tried to explain. "Remember Sir John Clifford, Angus? I had dinner
with him that night at the Red Lion Inn. When I lay
helpless on the wall at Berwick with an Englishman raising his sword to kill me, it was Sir John who saved my life."

"For that I give you thanks, Sir John," Angus said
gravely. "Are there any English left in the castle, Hugh?"

"None came in this door, Angus, but some might have
fled inside. In a dungeon beneath the great hall are four
Scots waiting to be released." Angus sent men to free
the Scots and turned to Sir John. "I will have to make
you a prisoner, but the men guarding you will be under
strict orders to protect you and see that you are decently
treated."

"Thank you, Angus Maclean."

Sir John was led away by two Highlanders and Hugh watched other English prisoners herded toward their own dungeons. "I watched it all from the battlements, Angus. It was a clever attack."

"It was Sir James Douglas planned and directed the fight, lad. Now it is almost finished. When the English race in from the hayfield they will be outnumbered three to one."

"But what of you, Angus? I thought you were killed in the river below Berwick!"

"Nonsense. I had a few arrows bounced off my head, but I was too busy fishing fallen Scots out of the water to be bothered with the English. You should have seen that boat! Full of Scots it was, with more clinging to the side as I rowed to safety. Many there were, lad, who told us of your battle on the wall. And quick they were to tell of your stand to Sir James Douglas. Gordon of Glenbirnie he will not soon forget."

Hugh sheathed his sword and went with Angus to meet the Scots who had so long shared his prison cell in Roslin Castle.

Bannockburn

On a black charger taken from the English stables at Roslin, Hugh rode with Sir James Douglas to the main Scots army, now stationed at Clackmannan Castle near Stirling, and presented himself to the king, who welcomed him heartily.

Then he went looking for Jock Lockhart, who was overjoyed to see him. "I have Sheila here in camp, lad. And sorry I was to leave you behind at Berwick. Some of our men who escaped said you had been killed on the wall. I thank God the report was untrue."

Hugh rushed happily off to the meadow outside the camp and found the black mare. Jock Lockhart grinned

as he watched the joyful reunion. "You think a lot of
Sheila, eh?"

"She reminds me of home, Jock. Now that I have
Sheila, I won't need any other horse. Do you have a
good one, Jock?"

"No, I'm afoot."

"You can have the charger I brought from Roslin. A
fine horse, Jock, but not like Sheila."

"Why, thanks, Hugh!"

The main army of the Scots lay close to Clackmannan
Castle during the winter months, keeping an eye on the
English garrison at Stirling. As spring approached, there
was a great activity in the Bruce's camp. Victories over
the English raised spirits among the Scots, who felt that
the year of 1313 would be a decisive one.

Riding back to the castle from his home in Galloway
early in April, Hugh reported to the Bruce's headquarters.
Later he encountered Jock Lockhart.

"I saw the king today, and he did not seem happy,
though most cordial. What's wrong, Jock?"

Jock looked grim. "The story in the army is that the
king's brother, Edward Bruce, has made a truce with the
English governor of Stirling Castle. 'Tis said the governor,
Sir Philip Mowbray, has agreed to surrender—if he is not
rescued by the midsummer of 1314!"

"No wonder the king is upset, Jock. A great English army
will undoubtedly invade Scotland to rescue Mowbray."

"Aye, King Robert is more than upset; he is furious. But
Edward is his favorite brother, and Edward has pledged
his word. There's nothing the Bruce can do but wait for
that English army to approach."

"Edward Bruce has not hurt us too badly," Hugh said.
"We can wait somewhere south of Stirling, perhaps along

that stream called Bannockburn. It is good country for
defense. To aid Mowbray, the English will have to fight
us there, and you know how stubborn our Scottish spearmen can be."

"Perhaps you're right, lad."

When Hugh reported at headquarters the next morning,
he found Angus Maclean sitting on a bench in the outer
room. The big Highlander called him over. "King Robert
has asked me to go south and scout the country. I have an
idea he'll want you to go along."

Angus was right. The king asked Hugh and Angus to
spend the rest of the year on the Border and in Galloway, keeping an eye on any unusually large concentra-
tion of English soldiers and reporting all troop movements.
They found Glenbirnie Castle an ideal headquarters for
their operations, since it was in a secluded spot in Galloway.

By February, Angus decided to move closer to the
Border. Hugh saddled Sheila and rode south with Maclean, into a cheerless drizzle which came down steadily.
For weeks they saw nothing, not even the sun. They
traveled by night and slept by day, until they reached the
road which led to Solway in England.

For days and weeks the pair lurked in the thickets
beside the road. They were cold and dismal, often hungry,
seldom dry. Hugh became impatient and discouraged. But
Angus insisted that they cross the Solway into English
territory, certain he would discover what he had been
sent to find.

They rode the river under cover of night and found a
clump of bushes on the English side. As the morning sun
rose, Angus, peering into the distance, looked at a great
treeless plain crowded with pavilions and tents. He

nudged Hugh. "There they are, lad. Now, use your eyes, Hugh Gordon. Tell me—what do you see?"

Hugh stood up, looking intently into the distance. Finally he spoke. "There are at least three thousand men-at-arms in that English camp, Angus. Those pavilions with the pennons flying are the quarters of the nobles, I'm sure. At least five hundred of Edward II's stoutest warriors."

"Your eyes are sharp," Angus said. "Perchance you see the English king himself in that camp."

Hugh looked again. "There is no Royal Standard there, Angus. But I cannot see all the pavilions. King Edward might well be there. I fear the English will send a great army against us sometime this year, these troops and others."

Cautiously they slipped away from the great English camp, riding through quiet country lanes to reach the Scottish side of the Solway, satisfied to have accomplished their mission but worried at the size of the English army.

"Angus, that is surely the greatest host which will ever be sent against Scotland. Saint Andrew protect our poor country!"

"It is not always might that counts, lad. Our king is one of the best generals in all Christendom. And our Scots will fight, on their legs if they can, on their knees if need be."

As spring came to the Border country, the English began to move slowly north, from Berwick to the Solway, with thousands of troops, nobles and knights, men-at-arms, archers. By day and night they marched toward Stirling, like a great snake uncoiling to strike.

In May, Hugh and Angus were watching from the hills above Lanark. To the south they could see a huge column of dust which seemed to blot out the sun. Then Hugh's sharp eyes caught the glint of the sun on mail and armor and lances. Slowly but steadily the English moved forward, men on spirited chargers, spearmen and bowmen on foot, wagon trains laden with provisions and tents.

Angus saw the army clearly as it rolled closer to Lanark. "They come amply fed and ready for war, lad. But perhaps they are soft and too well fed. A lean and hungry man fights better."

Quietly they walked back to their horses and rode across desolate moors and hills, circling around the English toward Edinburgh. As they galloped north, they met a troop of horses led by the restless Sir James Douglas. He shouted a greeting. "Well met, friends. What have you seen, Gordon, with those keen eyes?"

"A vast English army, Sir James, a few miles to the south and heading for Edinburgh. Where is His Highness?"

"Our main camp is close to Stirling Castle. While you ride back and join the Bruce, I'll look around and see if I can find out just when the English plan to attack."

Angus and Hugh reported to the king, who looked thoughtfully at his two ragged spies. "I thank you for the information, gentlemen," King Robert said. "How large is this force coming against us?"

"I think, sire," Hugh said, "that King Edward has at least sixty thousand men, counting levies from the Border English counties and units which joined him from Berwick. Wouldn't you say so, Angus?"

" 'Tis a fair estimate, Your Highness. We estimate that there are at least five thousand Welsh with the English, most of them archers, also a few Irish. Their cavalry is immensely strong. When we scouted them at the Solway, we saw men on huge chargers, men well appointed and equipped."

"Thanks again for your information. Angus, we will be

in battle soon. Will you fight with your Macleans? I am sure the chief of Clan Gillian will be glad to see you and your Lochaber ax once again.

"As for you, Gordon of Glenbirnie," the king went on. "I want you near me when the battle begins. I need your eyes, to watch troop movements at a great distance, to see just where our men need reinforcements. I do not want you in the forefront of battle, but as an aide. Is it understood?"

"Yes, sire."

It was a warm day in summer when the host of the English came up to St. Ninian's road, its flanks overlapping the main highway on both sides. From afar, Hugh watched the army move closer and closer, like a rising tide beating on the rocks of a Highland headland jutting out into the sea. He was awe-stricken as he watched that relentless march of fighting men.

Hugh turned Sheila around and galloped back to the place where the Bruce and his thirty thousand Scots were encamped, two miles south of Stirling Castle. When he reported that the English were swinging up St. Ninian's road which crossed the brook of Bannockburn and led directly to the Scottish positions, King Robert hastily deployed his men in line of battle, with three divisions prepared for instant action and a fourth in reserve.

The brook of Bannockburn ran directly across the front of the Scottish lines. For a mile or so, it could be forded by cavalry and foot soldiers, then its banks became high and steep, too steep for English men-at-arms on horseback. On the Scots side of the brook were bogs which were perilous to riders. Only in the center of the line could the English move forward with ease.

Inspecting his defenses with Hugh, King Robert pointed to the flat plain which ran down to the brook of Bannockburn. "This side of the stream, lad, our men have dug deep pits with stakes. Cavalry charging into those pits will fall through. Even foot soldiers will find it difficult to win their way out of that maze of traps."

"It is a wonderful defense system, Your Highness."

King Robert was sitting, erect in the saddle, on a small bay horse. He was wearing a thick leather helmet surmounted by his royal crown. Instead of mail, his body was covered with iron armor, legpieces, a form-fitting breastplate covering his chest, and a back piece. In his hand he carried a battle-ax instead of a sword.

Suddenly an English knight in full armor plunged his horse into the brook of Bannockburn and came out on the Scottish side. Beside him rode a bugler who blew lustily and announced in loud tones that Sir Henry de Bohun had come to challenge any knight in the Scots army to single combat.

As soon as de Bohun hurled his defiance, King Robert, ax in hand, rode slowly forward to meet the English invader. Hugh was appalled at the situation, for de Bohun carried a lance and was mounted on a powerful horse. The odds appeared to be heavily against the Scots king.

But before Hugh could ride to the Bruce's elbow and protest, he heard a rumble of hoofs behind him. Sir James Douglas in black armor dashed up, followed by a thickset man in mail, a stranger to Hugh. "His Highness is taking a foolish risk, Gordon."

"Aye, Sir James. But he rode away before I could prevail on him to avoid battle."

"Well, nothing can be done about it now. We'll have to watch the fray."

As the three anxious Scots sat their horses uneasily, de Bohun cantered out across the plain to meet the king, his lance down. Some twenty yards from the Bruce, he charged. As he approached, King Robert evaded the lance, ducking sideways in the saddle. Then he straightened himself up, battle-ax swung high in air.

With the power and grace of a born athlete, King Robert brought his ax crashing down on de Bohun's head as the Englishman, having missed with the lance, rode by. The blow stretched the English knight motionless on the ground, and a wild cheer rose from the Scots, to be followed by an anguished moan of many voices as King Robert himself fell to earth.

Sir James Douglas gripped Hugh's arm with iron fingers. "Gordon, what do you see? What has happened?"

"Nothing serious, sir. The ax haft broke in the king's hand as he struck the Englishman. The blow was so forceful that it stretched His Highness on the ground. See, he is getting up unhurt. It is the weight of his armor which encumbers him."

Sir James put spurs to his big black charger and galloped toward the king, with Hugh and the strange Scot pounding along a few paces behind. But before they reached him, the Bruce was back in the saddle as a wild shout of triumph rose from the Scottish lines.

"Your Highness," Douglas shouted, "you should never have taken such a risk, sire."

King Robert smiled slightly. "Douglas, 'tis a pity I broke the haft of my ax. It threw me off balance, and I was unhorsed, like a young squire."

"Thank God you are safe, sire," Hugh said feelingly.

As the Bruce rode back to the army, the stranger with Sir James turned to Hugh, holding out his hand. "We have not yet met, young sir. I am Randolph, Earl of Moray. The king's nephew."

"My name is Gordon, sir. Hugh Gordon of Glenbirnie."

"The Gordon who distinguished himself at Berwick! I have heard of you."

"I distinguished myself by getting captured, my lord."

"It could happen to anybody, Gordon. My uncle received a glowing report of your conduct at Berwick. He was worried when you disappeared, and most happy to learn you had survived."

The following day a large force of English cavalry rode forward in front of the Scottish lines, feeling out the Bruce's defensive positions, but the foot soldiers did not march to the attack.

A bugler summoned Hugh to King Robert's side. "Can you see what is taking place beyond the brook, Hugh? I stationed the Earl of Moray, my nephew, on the flank, to prevent the English from moving toward Stirling Castle. I am wondering if this parade of cavalry in front of us is a trick. It must be."

Hugh looked long into the distance. "Sire, there is a force of English cavalry circling around to the left, behind this force directly in front of us. I would say the horsemen are heading for the ground beyond St. Ninian's road."

"I knew it!" King Robert exclaimed. "That country in front of Moray is heavily wooded, and mayhap he does not see the threat to his force. Go quickly, Hugh, and warn him."

Hugh put spurs to Sheila and galloped away, angling back toward Stirling Castle. The mare was flecked with foam by the time he reached Moray and delivered his message. The king's nephew patted Sheila's heaving flank. "I thank you, Gordon, for the warning. Now we shall prepare a welcome for these English men-at-arms."

Hugh watched closely as Randolph of Moray arranged his Scots in battle formation. Since Moray had no cavalry, he drew up his foot soldiers in a hollow square. They were all pikemen, armed with long spears. The men in the front lines drove their spears, butt end, into the earth. Those in the second rank held their spears waist-high, projecting beyond the front line.

They had just a few minutes to wait before a trumpet blew in the ranks of the English cavalry and the earth trembled with the thud of horses down on that prickly array of spears, the hedgehog formation which the Scots called the "schiltron."

Hugh, sitting Sheila in the middle of the square, was awed by the thunder of the English cavalry attack, but Moray himself was cool and collected. "We shall beat them, Gordon. They will not drive their way inside the square. You will see!"

The hard-riding English men-at-arms struck savagely at the front line of Scots spearmen, but they could not drive their way inside the schiltron. For a time they milled about in front of the pikes, thrusting fiercely with sword and lance. Then the trumpet blew again, and the English recoiled, riding back to a small hill nearby.

"They will not try that again soon," Randolph of Moray shouted. "They've had enough."

The Earl of Moray was right, because the English sullenly rode back the way they had come. When they were out of sight Moray sent Hugh back to the king.

"Good news, that," the Bruce said as Hugh made his report. "Now the English will make the direct frontal attack. And our Scots foot soldiers will again show the world that spearmen can defeat heavily armed cavalry!"

The night before the Battle of Bannockburn, Sir James Douglas and Hugh rode quietly down to the stream which separated the Scottish and English armies. The water was running high, bank to bank, and Douglas was elated. "They can cross here, but they will pay dearly for it."

In the vast English camp on the south side of the brook, Hugh could hear the sound of feasting and drinking. Wild shouts crackled through the still night as drunken men boasted of the victory to come.

Sir James turned to Hugh. "They feel confident, since their army outnumbers ours two to one. They have at least ten thousand mounted men against our five hundred cavalry. They will be fighting under the eye of their king, yet they will lose, because they underrate the men they are about to fight. The English are like that, it is their greatest weakness."

They turned their horses around and rode quietly back to camp, carefully guiding their horses between the pits the Scots had dug to engulf the English cavalry.

On the warm morning of June 24, 1314, the Scots knelt and celebrated mass. The Scots army was vastly outnumbered. Many of the men had never fought a battle, raw recruits who had flocked to King Robert because they wanted Scotland to remain free. Hugh knew such volunteers had courage, but they were not well-trained soldiers.

As the day crept from the mists, they took up their positions in three divisions, well back from the brook of Bannockburn. Another division of Scots waited in reserve, behind the Bruce's standard, with the small force of cavalry.

The English came vigorously to the attack, thrusting at the right of the Scottish line. Their well-mounted men-at-arms rode fiercely forward, only to fall into the pits. The attacking cavalry were thrown into confusion, but English bowmen on foot moved up, sending a hail of arrows into the Scottish ranks.

As the Bruce's men were forced back, King Robert hastily summoned Hugh. "Go to Sir Robert Keith, quickly.

Tell him to circle around on the flank of those English archers and ride them down."

Hugh rode off to find Keith, who obeyed the king's instructions to the letter. The bowmen were dispersed, and the Scottish spearmen again re-formed their lines in the hedgehog formation, pikes bristling.

Dashing diagonally across the battlefield to reach the king again, Hugh saw another English division moving down into the wide brook, then another mass of men behind. As the two units forded the stream, the pennons of a hundred English nobles and knights fluttered in the breeze. Behind the nobility rode mailed men-at-arms, moving up the bank on the Scottish side. They were followed by serried ranks of archers, bowstrings taut and ready.

Hugh took up his position slightly behind King Robert, who was calmly surveying the battle scene from the hill. He watched closely as the Scottish hedge of spears held fast, throwing the English cavalry rudely back from the hedgehog formation.

The Bruce turned and beckoned to Hugh. "Notice, Gordon, that the English knights are so eager for glory that they have left their archers in the rear. They are between our Scots and the bowmen, which means that enemy cavalry itself is shielding our ranks from the arrow hail."

"I understand, sire."

"You have good eyes. Look behind the cavalry and tell me how many English have crossed Bannockburn, also the number pushing on behind them."

Hugh stood up in his stirrups and shaded his eyes, watching and counting. "There are a tremendous number of English on both sides of the brook, sire, but they seem to be confused, many of them wandering aimlessly around. I think it is because many of the men-at-arms have retreated back through the ranks of the archers."

"I have thrown three divisions into battle. Now is the time for the fourth division to fight." King Robert turned and waved to the general commanding the reserve division of Highlanders and Galloway men. "We shall remain here, Gordon, watching the battle from this hill. Be prepared to ride for any point in the battle line."

Hugh watched with pride as the Galloway men of the reserve division moved toward the center of the English line at a fast trot. Behind them came a wave of Highlanders, big men in bright kilts, each with a bullhide shield or target on his left arm, each with a sword in his right hand.

Straining his eyes, Hugh spotted Angus Maclean moving at the head of his clan, his Lochaber ax on his shoulder. He wondered where Jock Lockhart was, somewhere up front with the Galloway men.

Now the last units of the fourth division streamed by King Robert, bowmen running to reinforce the swordsmen who had already moved into the front line. As they passed the king and Hugh, they cheered, then dashed forward trying to overtake their comrades.

Meanwhile, the Galloway men had launched themselves on the English knights and men-at-arms, cutting and stabbing, hewing their way toward the brook of Bannockburn.

The horses of many English nobles and knights had fallen onto the stakes in the concealed pits. Some of the English cavalrymen, knights and men-at-arms alike, were lying on the ground where they had been thrown by frightened or wounded mounts.

The light-armed Galloway men moved over and across the line of English knights, throwing themselves on the

second English division of archers. As the Scottish swordsmen cut and slashed, the bowmen, unable to shoot down
their enemy at long distances, gave ground quickly, many
of them leaping into the brook of Bannockburn to escape
the furious Galloway attack.

Behind the Lowland Scots swept the tide of Highland
swordsmen and axmen. Many were bare to the waist, their
kilts flashing in the sun, their swords cutting and thrusting into what was left of the English cavalry. They swept
through the broken ranks and followed the Galloway men
into the brook, roaring their clan slogans.

"See, sire," Hugh said. "That last attack has driven the
English back across the brook. The Galloway men and
the Highlanders are fording the stream. They will soon
be on the far side, driving straight for the center of the
English line behind the brook."

"I cannot see that far, lad. Let us ride closer."

The Bruce put spurs to his horse and rode rapidly down
the hill, through the broken ranks of the English cavalry.
Nobles and knights lay on the ground side by side, the
pennons of a hundred famous English families drooping
beside the brook of Bannockburn. The king's face was
serious as he looked at the scene of death and desolation.
"A battlefield with dead and dying men is not a pretty
sight, Hugh Gordon. God rest all souls slain this day."

The Bruce turned to Hugh. "We have won a great
victory, lad. All of our advance divisions have moved forward and our reserves are deep in the English line. Get
you to Sir James Douglas at once and tell him to seize,
if possible, the person of Edward II, the King of England
but not of Scotland."

"Aye, Your Highness."

Hugh galloped toward St. Ninian's road, where he knew
the division under Douglas had driven the English right

wing back in disorder. He found Douglas shouting orders, urging his men south on the heels of the fleeing enemy. Finally, Hugh managed to make himself heard in the confusion. "The king, Sir James, thinks Edward of England is somewhere in the middle of the English line. He may be retreating now from the battle. He could be circling around to the right in an effort to reach the safety of Stirling Castle."

"Ha, I only wish he would go there, Gordon, since that fortress will soon be forced to surrender. I only have sixty horses, but I'll scout through the woods to the east of our position and see if I can locate the English king. Meanwhile Walter the Steward, my second in command, will continue to drive the English directly in front of us."

When Hugh went back to join King Robert, the battle was practically over. The English army, so self-confident and arrogant on that June morning, had almost ceased to exist.

"They are fleeing by the thousand," the Bruce told Hugh, "with our troops in hot pursuit. 'Tis a glorious day for Scotland, Hugh Gordon."

Hugh hesitated a second. "Your Highness, if you no longer have need of me, I crave your permission to ride down to the brook and search for Angus Maclean."

"Do so, by all means." King Robert's face was grave. "I hope nothing has happened to your friend. I am afraid many of our Highlanders are dead. You saw them on their way to battle, men without armor or mail."

Sheila picked her way carefully across the sloping battlefield. Hugh shaded his eyes from the June sun and looked carefully for signs of Angus. Here and there, Highlanders lay motionless among the English slain. They were no doubt dead, too, and Hugh felt suddenly sick.

Not all the Scots were dead. Now and then a man

groaned quietly in Gaelic, then lay quietly. Some of the Highlanders were bandaging their wounds and those of others. Once Hugh caught sight of the red and green Maclean tartan, but riding up, he saw the wounded man was not Angus.

Everywhere, he asked surviving Highlanders about Angus, but they spoke Gaelic only, and Hugh's knowledge of the language was so poor that he could not make them understand.

His hopes faded as he spurred Sheila down into the brook. In the middle of the stream, the mare was forced to swim a dozen yards, then found her footing again and climbed up the bank on the opposite side. Finally, as he rode on, he saw a little knot of men clustered around a Highlander lying on the ground. The tartan was red and green. Hugh looked sharply at the scene, and into the still, white face of Angus Maclean.

He dismounted heavily, his heart heavy with grief. "Is he dead, think you?"

A Galloway man standing by shook his head. "Say he is neither alive nor dead. This Highlander has lost a great deal of blood from a sword cut which bit deep. But he is sturdy and may well recover, young sir."

"Can you get a litter?" Hugh slipped a silver coin into the Galloway man's hand.

"Certainly, sir." The man looked at Hugh's stricken face. "God and Saint Andrew willing, your friend may soon be well again. I'll take him back to camp myself."

Hugh turned away, afraid the veteran soldiers would see his brimming eyes. Angus of the Ax, the man who had rescued him on the Dundee road, his companion on the scout to Berwick! The hero whose strength and courage had become a legend in North Scotland, lying there help- less and unknowing, between life and death!

Not so long ago, Hugh remembered, he had thought of war as a glorious adventure but, after seeing the face of Angus Maclean, he knew that war is a two-edged sword which cuts both ways, sparing neither the just nor the unjust.

Rise, Sir Hugh

Stirling Castle surrendered two days after Bannockburn, but Hugh could feel no glow of victory. He sat in the camp of the Macleans watching Black Angus, lying quiet and white like a man already dead.

Jock Lockhart, who had survived the battle, came to visit Hugh and looked gravely down at the unconscious Highlander. "I am truly sorry for the big man, Hugh. I know he is very dear to you."

"Thanks, Jock."

"I came to say good-by, lad. Sir James Douglas is leading an army to the Border, and he wants me along. There is still fighting to be done."

186

"Jock, I wish you well. If you are ever near Glenbirnie, stop in and visit old Thomas Dickson. He'll be glad to see you."

Jock mounted and rode away, and Hugh turned back to Angus. The big Maclean had lost so much blood that his body was strangely shrunken. Hugh knew his friend had had the best medical attention, for King Robert had sent his personal physician to care for Black Angus. Yet Hugh grieved to see a man once so full of life lying there like a helpless baby.

The next time the king's doctor called, Hugh had a long talk with him. "I'd like to move Angus to Galloway, where he'll be comfortable and quiet. Think you he can endure the journey?"

"In a litter, yes. If I were you, Gordon, I'd mention the trip to His Highness. Just as a matter of courtesy."

"Naturally. I am King Robert's man, whenever he has need of me."

A week later, Hugh rode Sheila up the long, winding road which led to Stirling Castle, where the king made his temporary headquarters. As he answered the challenge of the sentries at the gate and cantered into the inner courtyard, he could see stonemasons and carpenters and other artisans at work repairing and renovating the interior of the great fortress.

The Bruce, no longer in armor but dressed in a long robe with a rich fur collar, welcomed Hugh heartily. The Bruce seemed rested and relaxed, as if a great weight had been lifted from his broad shoulders.

Hugh told him of the conversation with the physician and asked permission to take Angus to Glenbirnie.

"I give my heartiest consent," King Robert said. "Stay with him at least six months and watch him well. Black

Angus has received a wound which would have killed an ordinary man.

"This," the king added, "you will be glad to hear. I have high hopes that Queen Marjory and the two princesses will be with me ere long. We are negotiating now for an exchange, the English Earl of Hereford for members of my family. And that is not all. I feel sure that our dear friend, the Countess of Buchan, will soon leave her Berwick prison and come back to Scots soil free once again."

"That is wonderful news, sire," Hugh said.

"I have something more to tell you, Hugh Gordon. For your great services to me, on the wall of Berwick and at Bannockburn, I intend to confer on you, a man of gentle blood, the order of knighthood."

Hugh tried to express his thanks, but the king lifted his hand. "I am not yet finished, my young friend. The order of knighthood is meaningless without property. Adjoining Glenbirnie is a huge manor owned by Sir Douglas MacDougall, always my enemy. That property, combined with your own estate, will produce a handsome income for your needs. It is yours, Gordon of Glenbirnie, because you chose to stand with me in my most desperate hours, instead of consorting with my enemies."

Speechless with gratitude, Hugh knelt before the Bruce. King Robert leaned forward and touched him gently on the shoulder. "Tomorrow night, you and five other young warriors will become knights in the great hall of Stirling Castle. After the ceremony, hasten to Glenbirnie with Angus Maclean, to whom I owe so much. But return to me again. I have need of your gifted eyes."

"That I will, Your Highness. My sword is ever at your service."

The following evening, Hugh again rode Sheila to Stirling Castle, ablaze with lights under the stars. Benches were arranged around the banquet tables in the great hall where King Robert and his nobles ate noble fare at a table on a raised platform.

Hugh sat beside Lord Kennedy, his companion in the dungeon at Roslin, who congratulated him on the honor he was soon to receive. He did not know what he was eating, realizing only that the servingmen were passing rich and tasty dishes before him, the like of which he had never seen, together with substantial fare like beef pies, mutton pasties, smoked salmon and wheaten bread.

At last the dinner was finished and the tables in the big hall were moved back. There, under the flickering candles in the wall sconces, Hugh stood up to be received as the trumpeters blew high, shrill, exciting notes.

Without armor, in long woolen hose which reached his thighs, an undertunic and close-fitting coat of pure white, Hugh marched solemnly to the king's table and knelt with the others on the edge of the dais.

King Robert, wearing the royal crown which the Countess of Buchan had placed on his head so many years ago, stood silently, his lips and eyes smiling, his sword in his hand. Slowly, he went down the line of candidates and, as he conferred the accolade, placing his sword blade lightly on each shoulder, he spoke the name of each young Scot in a voice which almost made the candles shake in their sconces.

When at last he came to Hugh, King Robert's voice was like a great bell. "With this, my sword of state, I dub thee knight," he said. "Rise, Sir Hugh."

The trumpets blew again and Lord Kennedy, Hugh's sponsor, attached the coveted golden spurs. Then the throng of nobles and knights surged forward to offer congratulations.

Finally the crowd quieted as King Robert approached.

Hugh started to kneel, but the Bruce stayed him. "Sir Hugh, you have my best wishes. I expect you back at my side when the snow flies, come Christmas."

"Thank you, sire. I shall be here."

Next morning Hugh started for Glenbirnie, riding Sheila, playfully grazing her flanks with the golden spurs. He was in a mail hauberk again, armed with sword and dagger. Behind him walked two ponies carrying between them a litter on which Angus Maclean lay.

Hugh turned and looked around at his small escort, six strapping Highlanders in mail shirts and kilts of red and green, four armed with bow and quiver, the other two carrying Lochaber axes. He smiled as the quiet peace of the Scots countryside enfolded him. He did not have to hurry. Glenbirnie would be waiting for him, nor did he have to scan the face of every man he met. There was no Englishman within two hundred miles.

They swung down the road toward Galloway. Hugh gave Sheila's bridle a gentle tug and waited for the litter to come alongside. "Angus, man of the Macleans, are you feeling better?"

"Well enough, Hugh. Sir Hugh, that is."

"We have already come a mile from Stirling Castle. Looking back just now at the tower, I saw, fluttering in the breeze, the Royal Standard of Scotland, with the Red Lion rearing on a field of yellow. 'Tis truly a glorious sight to see."

Black Angus' thin face broke into a smile. "A mile, and you can see the standard! Och, you have the gifted eyes, Gordon of Glenbirnie, and now you ride proudly, wearing the golden spurs. You have earned them, my friend. Not even Gillian of the Ax, the father of my clan, could have served King Robert as faithfully and well!"